FROM BE
AU
FRED MUSTARD ST
COMES HIS MOST
SHOCKING NOVEL YET . . .

STARCHILD

Books by Fred Mustard Stewart

Lady Darlington
The Mannings
The Methuselah Enzyme
Star Child
The Titan

Published by POCKET BOOKS

Most Pocket Books are available at special quantity discounts for bulk purchases for sales promotions, premiums or fund raising. Special books or book excerpts can also be created to fit specific needs.

For details write the office of the Vice President of Special Markets, Pocket Books, 1230 Avenue of the Americas, New York, New York 10020.

STAR CHILD

FRED MUSTARD STEWART

PUBLISHED BY POCKET BOOKS NEW YORK

This novel is a work of fiction. Names, characters, places and incidents are either the product of the author's imagination or are used fictitiously. Any resemblance to actual events or locales or persons, living or dead, is entirely coincidental.

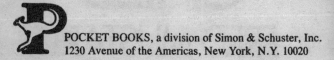

POCKET BOOKS, a division of Simon & Schuster, Inc.
1230 Avenue of the Americas, New York, N.Y. 10020

Published by arrangement with Arbor House Publishing Co.
Library of Congress Catalog Card Number: 74-80712

ISBN: 0-671-54357-1

First Pocket Books printing August, 1986

10 9 8 7 6 5 4 3 2 1

POCKET and colophon are registered trademarks
of Simon & Schuster, Inc.

Printed in the U.S.A.

As always,
to Joan.
And to Don Fine,
a master at his craft.

CONTENTS

*"Si Dieu n'existait pas
il faudrait l'inventer."*
*("If God did not exist, it would
be necessary to invent him.")*
—VOLTAIRE

PART I

The Annunciation

1

The seventeen-year-old blonde giggled as the man with the owl head led her down the wooden steps into the cellar.

"So *this* is your big secret?" she said, looking around. "But what is it?"

"It's my chapel," he replied. He was tall, and he wore a black opera cloak around his body. The owl-head mask covered his entire head. It was made of white feathers, and the big owl eyes had small holes pierced in them through which he was watching her. He held a half-gallon bottle of Almadén Chablis and an empty glass. Her glass was half full, and she was sipping as she looked at the altar at the end of the room.

"A private chapel. That's a kicky idea." She leaned over and kissed the beak of the owl mask. "I had no idea you were so creative. But what's it a chapel *to?*"

"The Great God Raymond," he said.

She snickered.

" 'Raymond'? That's a dumb name for a god."

"No dumber than Jesus," he replied, setting the bottle of wine on the dirt floor. The cellar was old: the ceiling beams swayed with age and dry rot, and the stone walls looked as if they dated from the late eighteenth or early nineteenth century. At the end opposite the small altar, an enormous coal furnace squatted in the semidark, its steel-vent tentacles spreading in all directions like an octopus.

"Well, I think it's a good idea to have your own god," she said as she plopped on the steel cot in the center of the cellar, bouncing up and down on its squeaky springs. The naked light bulb above her spilled its light on her short golden hair. She had California-style good looks, with a beautiful figure that was covered with a white terrycloth bathrobe. Her legs and feet were bare. The owl eyes watched her from the bottom step.

"Is this the altar where we make love to Raymond?" she asked, almost spilling her wine on the white sheets as she bounced.

"Sort of."

"Ben, you're wild, and I love it! I had no idea all this was down here. Take off that silly mask and come here and kiss me. Then tell me all about Raymond. Maybe I'll join the church."

He lifted off the owl mask and set it on a low, wooden blanket chest against the wall. Then he ran his fingers through his hair, which was as blond as hers. He was eighteen, and he was handsome.

He spread out the black opera cloak, revealing that he had on nothing but a pair of blue briefs. Then he swooped down on her, yelling in a Bela Lugosi accent, "I am Drrra-cula! And I come to drrrink your blood!"

He enveloped her in his cloak as he leaned down and sank his teeth into her neck. She ran her hands around his sides, rubbing his smooth skin.

"Mmmm. It's half-wine, but it's all yours."

He brought his mouth up to hers, and they kissed. She felt his lips open and his tongue push out. She opened her mouth, and their tongues darted at each other like angry snakes. She felt his hands inside her bathrobe on her naked breasts, and she wanted him more than ever before. She tried to pull him down on top of her, but he resisted.

"Oh Ben," she whispered, *"now . . ."*

"No, that's not the way Raymond wants it."

"Well, screw Raymond!" she snapped, sulkily, as he straightened and went over to get the wine. He filled his glass and took a drink. Then he turned.

"Raymond is the new god who's coming to earth soon to bring mankind a new religion—a wonderful new religion that worships the body, not the soul."

She smiled, her good humor returning. He was, after all, putting on a terrific show.

"I like *that* kind of religion a lot better than the others."

"So do I. You see, Raymond started coming into my dreams about a week ago. At first, it sort of scared me . . ."

"What does he look like?" she interrupted.

"He can look like anything he chooses. Sometimes he's a beautiful woman, sometimes he's a beautiful man . . . he can be a goat or a lizard. One night he even became an owl."

She laughed and pointed at the owl mask.

"So *that's* why . . ."

He nodded.

"That gave me the idea. Anyway, Raymond is all-powerful and all-knowing. And when he arrives in our world, it will be the beginning of a new age of love and joy . . . and some other things."

"It sounds wonderful! I love this fantasy. This is your best one yet."

He smiled slightly.

"Good. I'm glad you like it." He took off his opera cloak and tossed it on the blanket chest. "You see, Raymond taught me that the act of love must be an act of worship too. Because each time we make love, we expend part of the psychic force of the universe. So he told me to build an altar to him and to Starfire." He held out his hand. She got off the cot to join him.

"Who's Starfire?"

"That's Raymond's father. Starfire is the Creator."

He led her to the altar. It was a wooden chest draped

15

with a black silk shawl fringed with gold. Two brass candlesticks stood on it with a white bowl between them. A box of kitchen matches and two black half-masks rested behind the bowl. He picked up the box of matches, pulled one out and struck it.

"The candles," he said, as he lighted them, "represent Raymond . . . and this one is Starfire."

"What's in the bowl?"

"Myrrh and frankincense."

"Where'd you get it?"

"In Fairfax. It cost a bundle."

He lighted the incense, which began smoking, permeating the cellar with its perfume. He put back the matchbox, tossing the dead match on the floor. Then he picked up the two half-masks and held one out to her.

"Here: put this on."

"Why?"

"It's part of the ritual. By hiding part of our faces from each other, we concentrate more on our bodies."

She looked dubious, but she took the mask and stretched the elastic over her hair.

"It's tight," she complained.

He had put on his mask also.

"But doesn't it make it different?"

"Yes," she admitted. "It's weird, but it does make it sexier."

He put his hands on the collar of her bathrobe.

"Now we must consecrate our bodies," he whispered.

He gently opened the robe. She relaxed as he removed it from her, letting it drop to the floor at her feet. Her full breasts and flat stomach glowed in the light of the candles. He put his arms around her and pulled her to him, brushing his lips against hers. She reveled in the warmth of his muscled body.

"I consecrate your body to Raymond," he said, softly. "And my body to Starfire."

"What am I supposed to say?" she whispered, her eyes closed.

"Nothing. You're only supposed to feel and enjoy. And then the spirit of Raymond will flow through you."

She kissed his shoulder, then lay her head on it, putting her arms around his narrow waist. "I love you, Ben," she said. "You're so beautiful."

"You must love Raymond, too."

She looked up and smiled.

"All right. I'll love him, too."

He gently removed her arms from around him, then led her back to the cot.

"Lie down," he whispered, kissing her. She obeyed as he reached up to pull the chain and turn out the light bulb. Now the cellar was dark except for the soft glow of the candles.

He pulled down his briefs and kicked them free. Then, naked, he straddled her on the cot. She opened her arms to him, and he leaned down to kiss her.

She felt the tip of his warm, stiff penis bump her stomach. Then he placed it in her vagina and began thrusting. She moaned softly as the sweetness mounted inside her.

And then they both came.

When it was over, he lay beside her. She stared up at the dark ceiling, a smile on her face.

"It was beautiful," she whispered. "You make me so happy, Ben."

His right arm reached for something under the cot. It was a butcher knife he had stuck between the springs and the mattress.

"*Raymond* makes you happy."

She laughed.

"You nut," she said, affectionately. "How do you get all these crazy ideas?"

He sat up, holding the knife behind his back.

"It's not crazy. Raymond is real. He's the son of

Starfire, and his arrival on earth has been heralded in my dreams."

"Be *serious,*" she said, with a hint of annoyance. "And what are you doing?"

He had straddled her and was looking down at her, the knife still behind his back.

"I am the first apostle of the new religion," he whispered. "And I consecrate you as my first sacrifice to Raymond."

"What?"

She stared at the butcher knife as he brought it around and raised it above her chest.

"Ben . . ."

The knife flashed down and buried itself in her heart. Blood squirted up like a broken water main.

She died instantly.

The town of Shandy shimmered in the late-August sun, which had sent the thermometer to a sizzling (by New England standards) 96 degrees, as Helen Bradford came out of the one grocery store in town carrying a paper sack filled with price-inflated food. Shandy, which was in the northwest corner of Connecticut just a few miles south of Massachusetts, was ringed by the Berkshire foothills and straddled the lovely Housatonic River, so its natural setting was hard to improve upon. The town itself was no architectural gem, although the white Congregational church, built in the 1860s, was a handsome example of Victorian Gothic (if one liked Victorian Gothic), and there were a few pleasant Colonial houses along Route 9, which doubled as Shandy's main street. The shopping district was less than a block long and consisted of Grayson's Hardware Store, the Shandy Package Store (a good selection of wines), Haley's Market, two or three antique shops and the Shandy Soda Shoppe where one could buy greasy hamburgers and *The New York Times.* Across the railroad tracks (no longer used: the train station had been converted into a candle shop) lay the pseudo-Colonial drug store and the laundromat; opposite the Congregational Church was Dryer's Real Estate Office.

In the other direction, south of the Civil War Memorial column erected in 1883, was the town hall and two gas stations. And that, with the exception of the school and the cemetery, was all there was to Shandy, population 267. At least in the summer. But already the tiny town was preparing itself psychologically for the opening of the school three weeks away, at which time over four hundred boys and girls from all over the country would descend on the handsome pseudo-Georgian campus across the river and more than double the town's population. Shandy Prep, as it was called, was one of the top private schools in the East. It was Shandy's biggest source of tax revenue and premier (and almost only) employer, its faculty of forty all living in or near the town.

Jack and Helen Bradford were unusual in that they were the only husband-and-wife team on the faculty.

As she climbed into her Toyota in front of Haley's Market, Helen thought about her husband and the second anniversary party they were throwing the next night (for which she had just bought a leg of lamb). Two years married, and she was still as much in love with Jack as she had been that summer two years before when they had defied the town gossips by living together for six weeks before tying the knot that didn't seem to bind for very long any more. But theirs was holding. She was not only still in love with her husband, she actually *liked* him—and this despite his moodiness, his occasional bursts of temper, his nail-biting, his habit of watching old movies on the Late Show which kept her awake till two in the morning, and his getting drunk at parties. Oh well . . . She supposed she had a list of faults, too. On the plus side, he was usually thoughtful, he was physically exciting (she still loved to look at him when he was naked), he was good in bed (and these days, that was no minor achievement: he was actually normal, though lately he had been trying some, well, experiments), he was bright and could be funny, and he was a terrific teacher: the best in the English department. His students adored him, and so did she. As she drove across the Housatonic and passed the empty campus (not entirely empty: she saw Jeremy and Marcia Bernstein playing tennis on one of the school courts), she told herself she had a lot to be thankful for.

She had turned twenty-eight the previous June. She was tall, and while she was no beauty by conventional standards, her fine complexion, lovely chestnut hair and big, expressive green eyes customarily earned her the description of "awfully attractive." She was from Wiscasset, Maine, where her father still worked as an executive for the Bath Iron Works, but four years at Vassar had softened her Maine accent. Spending her junior year in France, she fell in love with the country, the culture and the language and returned after college for graduate work at the Sorbonne. Three years before, she had accepted a position in the Shandy French department, the same year Jack Bradford joined the English department. Vassar-Sorbonne-Maine fell in love with St. Marks-Harvard-Boston on their second date.

Her car was rattling up the steep Rock Mountain Road; now she turned in the driveway of their rented house and parked in front of the double garage. Jack, dressed in nothing but khaki shorts and filthy tennis shoes, was following the gas mower around the small front lawn that overlooked a breathtaking view down the mountain of the town and school and river in the valley below. Seeing his wife, he turned off the mower and ran his arm across his mouth—despite the handkerchief tied around his forehead, his face was dripping with sweat. He was six-foot-four, too lean, with the lanky grace of a swimmer, which he had been at Harvard. His long dark-brown hair was streaked copper by the sun, and his narrow, tanned face and what she thought of as his wild brown eyes gave him the look of a superannuated hippie, which in a way he was. In the Sixties, Jack Bradford had dropped out for a while, turned on, and tried to make art films. He had failed; he was now married and thirty-two; besides, it was the Seventies. He hated to admit it, but Jack Bradford had been Establishmentized.

"What'd you buy?" he asked as she got out of the car.

"A gorgeous leg of lamb."

"To hell with the budget. Did you get the wine?"

She rolled her eyes.

"Damn. I forgot."

"Well, I'll get it this afternoon. Hot, isn't it?"

"Like an oven." She was carrying the groceries to the kitchen door when she heard a muffled thud from the top of the mountain. She looked up to see one of the tall white pines that crowned Rock Mountain bounce on its side.

"Who's cutting the pines?" she asked.

"Ben. Says he's going to sell them for firewood."

"But that's a shame! Those gorgeous trees . . ."

"It's his mountaintop, baby. How about making el slave-o some iced tea?"

He was looking at her rather defiantly, as if cutting short any further discussion of Ben Scovill or his trees. It rather annoyed her.

"All right."

Taking a final look up the mountain, she went into the cool kitchen to put away the groceries and mix the instant Lipton. Ben Scovill, their nearest neighbor over the top of the mountain. Nice Ben, Handsome Ben, Friendly Ben: why did she always get her back up when he was mentioned? The Scovills were one of the oldest local farm families, their hundred-acre farm on the north face of Rock Mountain having been in the family for five generations. This made Ben a "townie," the term used with semiconscious snobbery by the school faculty to describe the low-income natives, yet he had won a scholarship to Shandy Prep, which put him in an ambiguous straddling-two-worlds category that he had adjusted to well. Ben was bright and a fine athlete. Everyone liked him; Jack liked him enormously. Ben had gone out for the school swimming team, which Jack coached, and swiftly under his tutelage he had become a first-rate diver. The combination of their athletic relationship with the fact that they were neighbors had created a bond between them that Helen thought was unwise between teacher and student: friendship yes, but "buddies" never. Jack had disagreed. And the death of Ben's father from a brain tumor the previous May had added a dimension of protectiveness to Jack's feeling since Ben's mother had died six years before in a car accident and the young man was now alone in the world. Jack and Ben. She wasn't sure why she couldn't share her husband's enthusiasm for him, but there *was* a remoteness she sensed in him that didn't seem to come from shyness—he was anything but shy—but rather, she thought, from slyness. She never quite knew what he was thinking, which bothered her. She knew it was unfair for her to dislike him for something as vague as that, particularly since apparently she was the only person who felt as she did. Sometimes she even asked herself if she weren't perhaps a bit jealous of him, as if she somehow resented sharing her husband. But that was irrational. She wasn't sharing Jack with Ben. Still, the feeling was there: vague, unstated, but there.

And now he was cutting down his trees for firewood. An innocent enough act, she realized, but Jack's seemingly curt refusal to discuss it gave it an almost conspiratorial air. A conspiracy? Over cutting down a tree? She was imagining things, she told herself. And yet as she stirred the iced tea in the glass pitcher she couldn't convince herself that the pines were being cut down merely for firewood.

There was something else to it? . . .

* * *

That night she had the first dream.

She found herself in a beautiful valley. Through the center ran a small stream that sparkled like sequins beneath the blazing sun, and lovely green fields stretched to the distant hills. Ahead of her was an apple tree in full white blossom, and she found herself drifting toward it. As she came closer, she saw that there was someone standing beneath it. It was a boy, about ten years old, she judged, with beautiful golden hair and the face of a Botticelli angel. He was wearing a short white tunic, his arms, legs and feet bare, and she became aware that she too was wearing a white robe of the same gossamer material. As she came up to him, he spread his arms in a welcoming gesture and smiled.

"I am Star Child," he said simply.

She sat on a big rock and stared at him.

"Don't be afraid," he continued, lowering his arms. "I mean you no harm. I've thought-projected myself into your sleeping mind so that we can learn to trust each other."

"Thought-projected? . . ."

"My people have developed a way to project our thoughts out of our physical brains into the brains of others. We do it by mechanically generating an electromagnetic field which we use to transmit thought through space. You may think of it as a highly sophisticated version of your radio transmission."

"Why did you—whoever 'you' are—why did you develop it?"

He hesitated.

"For reasons I won't go into now," he answered evasively. "They are reasons that would sound ugly to you, and I don't want you to think of me as ugly. You see, because our race has evolved somewhat differently from yours, thanks to our slightly different environment, I've assumed the shape of one of your children so that you won't find me alien or frightening. We know you tend to trust your children—rightly or wrongly—and as I said, I want you to trust me as I must trust you. Later I will reveal myself in my true form. You may be surprised to find that I'm not all that different from you, after all."

"But . . ." She was so confused, she hardly knew what to ask first. ". . . where are you from?"

"Our world is a medium-sized planet revolving around the star your astronomers call 'Tau Ceti.' Our sun is similar to yours. However, our race evolved much sooner in time than your race. We are technologically far advanced over you: the reason we know this is that we have monitored your civilization for several thousand years. We know that your civilization is in a time of great peril, which is why I have been sent to your planet. I bring with me a gift of incalculable importance to your world, a gift that will alter your history. But . . ." He paused, and for the first time she noticed a look of fear come into his eyes. Until then his face had seemed divinely impassive and benign. Now, suddenly, he looked very human, like a troubled child. "There is someone who is trying to destroy my mission. Have you had other dreams lately? Has someone else come into your mind?"

"No. I mean, I don't *remember* any dreams . . ."

"You would remember it if it happened, as you'll remember this. He may try to thought-project into your mind."

"Who?"

Star Child hesitated.

"It doesn't matter now, but it *may.*"

She was becoming exasperated.

"Why are you being so mysterious?" she asked impatiently. "What's this 'gift' you're bringing us? Why is our civilization in any more peril now than it usually is?"

He looked at her closely.

"It's important my mission to your world be known only to a handful. For that reason, you must swear to tell no one of this dream-encounter, or what I tell you, until I instruct you to do otherwise. Will you swear?"

She shrugged helplessly.

"I don't think anyone would believe me anyway."

"That doesn't matter: you must still swear to tell no one. Will you do so?"

"Well, I suppose . . ."

"Swear not on your god, but on your love of your fellow man."

She frowned. The intensity of his tone was dispelling her disbelief.

"Yes, I swear," she said quietly.

Star Child seemed to relax.

"Good." He sat down on the grass next to her and looked up into her face. "Your world is becoming aware it's running out of power, that your supplies of fossil fuels are limited. Have you ever heard of controlled thermonuclear fusion?"

"No," she answered, feeling almost guilty for not having heard of it.

"That's not surprising: few of you are aware of it. Your scientists are, though. They're desperately trying to find a way to generate it, because they know it's the ultimate power source, the one thing that can save your planet from becoming a dead world. They're years away from its secret, though."

"I still don't know what it is. Are you talking about the hydrogen bomb?"

"No, I'm talking about the power source of your sun. I'm talking about a limitless supply of energy that would be cheap and relatively nonpolluting. Your hydrogen bombs are crude devices that depend on uncontrolled thermonuclear fusion for their destructive power. But if you could control the power, it would mean the greatest revolution in the history of your civilization since the harnessing of electricity—perhaps of all time. All the energy requirements of your entire planet for a whole year could be generated from fuel held on one barge in New York harbor. It would mean the end of world poverty, the end of most wars—which are usually caused by poverty—and, most important, the end of the pollution of your air and water. And that's the gift I'm bringing your world: the technology to achieve controlled thermonuclear-fusion power *now*."

Though she didn't fully understand what he was saying, she understood enough to be stunned by its implications.

"But why are you giving it to us?" was all she could think of to ask.

He smiled.

"You're suspicious: that's to be expected. Let's merely say that brotherhood exists elsewhere in the universe, not only in your world—though it's rare enough there. We're helping you because we don't want you to destroy yourselves, as you surely will when your present power sources begin to dwindle. But again I must insist you tell no one of these things: *no* one. You *do* understand that?"

"Yes . . ."

He looked reassured.

"Good. You have been chosen by me to play a great role in the history of your civilization. Do not betray my trust."

And with that, to her amazement, he began to fade from view. She got to her feet.

"Wait a minute . . . don't go . . ."

"I will return," he whispered, his voice as transparently thin as his body had become. "Meanwhile, remember your vow."

And then he vanished, and she was alone in the valley. A breeze stirred the branches of the apple tree as she looked around her, trying to understand where she was.

And then she woke up.

She was in her bed, next to her husband, in their second-floor bedroom. She sat up and rubbed her head, which was splitting. Then she looked at the luminous dial of the alarm clock on the bed table. Three twenty-five. Now she remembered. They had gone up to bed at ten, made love, then—with a bumpy return to the prosaic—Jack had turned on Channel Four news. At eleven-thirty he switched channels to watch, for the umpteenth time, *Dark Victory* with Bette Davis and George Brent. Defying the sound track, she had finally drifted off to sleep about one, just when Bette Davis found out she was going to die. "Prognosis negative" had been the last line of dialogue she remembered.

And then the dream.

It was certainly the strangest one she had ever had. She rarely dreamed—or rarely *remembered* dreaming—but as Star Child had predicted, she remembered this one in vivid detail, almost as if she had been talking to the angelic boy in that very room. She had never dreamed in color, but she remembered his white-gold hair, the blue of the sky, the green of the grass. And the smell of the apple blossoms. She was certain she had never *smelled* anything in her dreams before, but she remembered the fragrance.

And "Tau Ceti." She had never heard of a star called Tau Ceti. She must have made the name up—or rather, her subconscious must have made it up. But what a weird name! And "controlled thermonuclear fusion"? Why in God's name would she dream about that?

She felt Jack's hand touch her arm, and she realized he was awake too.

"What's wrong?" he said.

"Nothing. I just had a weirdo dream."

Silence for a moment. Then he sat up and turned on the bed lamp.

"What kind of dream?"

Do not betray my trust. . . .

"Oh, I forget. It was silly. Would you get me two aspirin? The wine at dinner's given me a gorgeous headache."

Liar, she thought as he climbed out of the big four-poster that had come with the house and went in the bathroom. You only had two glasses of Beaujolais. It wasn't the wine, it's that goddam dream . . . or thought projection? . . . Was it possible it really wasn't a dream? . . .

That, of course, was crazy. And yet . . . she had obeyed Star Child's instruction. She hadn't told the dream to her husband. She had wanted to, but she hadn't. Strange . . .

He came back with a glass of water and two aspirin, which she took as he sat next to her, watching her.

"Raymond," he said quietly.

"What?"

"The dream. Was it about someone named 'Raymond'?"

She frowned.

"Who's Raymond?"

He looked at her for a moment, searching her eyes.

"Then it wasn't Raymond?"

"No."

"I thought you said you'd forgotten what it was about."

"I have, but I remember what it *wasn't* about. And it wasn't about someone named Raymond."

"But I heard you say it in your sleep."

"What?"

" 'Raymond.' You said the name 'Raymond.' "

She looked totally baffled. He shrugged and lay back down, pulling the sheet up to his waist as he said, "Oh well, it doesn't make any difference. Good night."

He turned out the light.

"Good night, darling."

She put the glass on the table, then lay down, wondering who the hell Raymond was. A slight breeze puffed down the mountain into the north window, cooling their bodies as it passed over the bed to escape out the south window. Then she whispered, "Jack?"

"Huh?"

"Did you ever hear of something called controlled thermonuclear fusion?"

"No. What the hell's that?"

"Did you ever hear of something called 'Tau Ceti'?"

"Tau who?"

"Ceti."

"What's Tau Ceti? A new Greek wine?"

"No. It was . . ." Careful. "I seem to remember that being in the dream."

"Then you'd better start dreaming in subtitles. That doesn't make any sense."

"I know."

She dropped the subject, listening to his deep breathing, which quickly grew deeper as he slipped off into sleep. Her mind was whirling with confusion, but soon she too began to feel drowsy.

In ten minutes, she had fallen asleep.

Though Dr. Norton Akroyd practiced psychiatry in a part of the world where violent crime was almost unheard of (Shandy's last-known killing had occurred in 1923), the forty-year-old bachelor was fascinated with murder. Not only fascinated; he was known as something of an expert on it, having written a book called *The Psychosexual Basis of Murder* that had become almost a classic in its field. In it Norton had argued that the potential for murder exists in every human being but that the killing instinct is not a product of rage or hate alone (though they may be present) so much as an extension of the sexual urge: that murder is pleasant, just as sex is pleasant, and that to the murderer the killing can produce an exaltation that is as gratifying—if not more so—than the sexual orgasm.

When the book had come out the year before, its rather sensational thesis had caused a stir on the quiet campus of Shandy Prep, where soft-spoken Norton

Akroyd was the resident psychiatrist and head of the small psychology department, and jokes had spread around the school about mild-mannered Norton Akroyd stepping, Clark Kent–fashion, into a phone booth to strip off his understated tweeds and emerge Superkiller, hot on the spore of his blood-prey. For a time, some of the more fuddy-duddy faculty wives viewed Norton rather nervously and twitched when they found themselves next to him at faculty teas, fantasizing lurid rape-murders in their heads. All this Norton viewed with private amusement, and, as he knew it would, the sensation soon died down. He was, after all, liked and respected by both the faculty and the students. He frequently speculated, though, about what the school's nervous Nellies would think if they saw the living room of his three-room apartment in Miller Hall, one of the red-brick pseudo-Georgian dormitories on campus. Norton was researching a new book, a follow-up on his first one, which was to be a history of famous murderers, and his big steel desk was piled with tomes on Gilles de Raïs, Sawney Bean, the Bavarian ripper, Lacenaire, Karl Hussman, Jack the Ripper, Leopold and Loeb, Richard Speck, the Dusseldorf Vampire . . . it was a treasure trove of gore, and in his steel file cabinet next to the desk was even more: photographs of victims, hard-to-come-by books on forensic medicine, compilations of crime statistics. . . .

The afternoon after Helen's dream, as he put on his neatly pressed searsucker jacket preparing to go to the Bradfords' house for their anniversary dinner, he glanced at his desk and decided to file the glossy photo of a recent Boston rape-stabbing victim he had received in the mail that morning from a friend on the Boston police force. There were a number of workmen around the campus preparing the school for its opening, and one never knew when one might come into the apartment by mistake and see the picture. Norton Akroyd didn't like to encourage rumors.

He filed the photo, left the apartment, got in his black Mercury and drove through the pleasant campus to Rock Mountain Road. There had been a thunderstorm that noon which had broken the heat wave, and now the weather was cool and the sky clear—a perfect evening for the Bradfords' party, he reflected. Norton was fond of Helen and Jack Bradford, even though Helen's unsubtle attempts at matchmaking sometimes got on his nerves. For instance, he knew that Helen had invited Sarah Blake to the party that night to "balance off" Norton. Sarah, who was the assistant head of the music department and the school organist, was attractive and interesting, but she was heavily into women's lib, which was all right with Norton, who agreed with much the movement stood for, except that Sarah kept talking about it, which was a bore. The prospect of an evening of female chauvinism wasn't exactly exhilarating, but there was no way around it. He wondered if he should tell Helen outright he liked being a bachelor and would she please forget trying to pair him up, but decided tonight was not the appropriate time for such bluntness.

He pulled into the driveway of the Bradfords' genuine Colonial house and parked next to the headmaster's gray Mercedes. The house, which Jack rented from a retired teacher whom arthritis had forced to Florida, was a white clapboard, black-shuttered ex-farmhouse that had been built in the 1840s. A double garage and modern kitchen had been added, but essentially the house retained its sturdy Colonial dignity, perched, as it was, on a ledge below the top of Rock Mountain with its gorgeous southern view. Norton admired the house and envied the Bradfords' luck at getting such a gem for only three hundred dollars a month rent, furnished.

The door was opened by Helen, who looked smashing in a long white skirt and green blouse. She kissed him as he handed her the bottle of champagne he had bought for their anniversary, then led him into the long, low-ceilinged white living room with the hand-some fieldstone floor. Aside from Lyman Henderson, the corpulent headmaster of the school, and his gray-haired wife, Marjorie, the other guests were Jeremy and Marcia Bernstein and tall, intense Sarah Blake. To Norton's surprise and delight, Sarah wasn't talking women's lib. Rather, the topic was crime.

"Here's our murder maven!" said Jeremy, a bearded colleague of Jack's in the English department whose specialty was the modern novel. "Norton, have you solved the mystery?"

"What mystery?" asked the psychiatrist, accepting a glass of white wine from Jack. Norton drank nothing but wine.

"Judy Siebert. Haven't you heard? She's disap-peared."

"Who's Judy Siebert?"

"That cute blond trick that works at the Soda Shoppe in town. Her father, Art Siebert, owns it. She vanished last Wednesday night, and no one knows what happened to her."

"But Jeremy, don't you think you're jumping to a few conclusions thinking she's been murdered?" said Marjorie Henderson, who had a Long Island lockjaw accent that matched her patrician face. "Maybe she just ran away. If Art Siebert were my father, *I'd* run away."

Her fat husband chuckled.

"She probably ate one of Art's greasy hamburgers and died of food poisoning."

"I think you're all assuming Judy was acted *on,*" said Marcia Bernstein, Jeremy's dark, attractive wife who had grown up on Central Park West and hated Shandy's rural placidity with the same intensity she missed New York's urban excitement. "If you ask me, Judy's perfectly capable of getting herself in trouble."

"Why?" asked Jack, joining the group with his second martini. "She seems like a nice girl."

"Oh, come *on*," said Marcia. "She's a little tramp. She sleeps with half the lacrosse team."

"What's wrong with the other half?" asked Lyman, who was accustomed to Marcia's cynicism and didn't believe her Peyton Place view of the town and his school.

"They're waiting in line. I'll bet five dollars Judy got bored and took off for New York for some kicks."

"Maybe she got pregnant?" suggested Marjorie Henderson.

Marcia laughed. *"No* one gets pregnant any more, Marjorie. You're dating yourself. Even in Shandy they've got the pill."

"Well, *I* say she's murdered," declared Jeremy, who was thirty-one and had a handsome, if heavily pockmarked face. "I guess she got picked up by a hitchhiker who raped her and buried her body in a field. What do you think, Norton?"

The psychiatrist shrugged.

"Who knows? You've all read my book: you know I think anyone's *capable* of murder. But I have to admit I think it's fairly unlikely anyone's murdered Judy. People in Shandy don't seem very interested in killing each other, which I'll admit doesn't say much for the accuracy of my book's thesis."

"Norton, you really do know how to cheer people up," said Helen, nervously eyeing her husband, who had just finished the second martini. She didn't want him tackling the third. "And though I know you'd all rather talk gore, it *is* our anniversary, and dinner is ready, so shall we go in the dining room and forget Judy Siebert?"

They followed her into the small dining room, where Helen had set a lovely table, using the Quimper plates she had bought in France and the glass dolphin candlesticks she'd bought from the Metropolitan Museum's Christmas catalogue, but they didn't forget Judy Siebert. Rather, Marcia Bernstein, who was seated next to Norton, if for no other reason than to annoy Helen, continued talking on the subject. Marcia liked to annoy Helen.

"Do you really believe what you wrote in that book?" she said, spooning her jellied madrilène. "I mean about murder being a sex kick?"

"I didn't say that exactly," replied Norton. "I said there is a sexual basis for murder. That murder is pleasurable to the murderer."

"Well? Isn't that saying murder is a sex kick?"

The psychiatrist sighed.

"All right, but no author likes having three hundred pages of his deathless prose reduced to one cliché."

"Perhaps *some* murderers kill for pleasure," said Lyman Henderson across the table, his round, bald head barely visible over the big plant of yellow chrysanthemums from Helen's garden. "But I disagree with your idea that every murder is pleasurable. There are murders of revenge, murders for profit, casual murders . . ."

"What's a 'casual' murder?"

"A killing that takes place during a robbery, for instance. The thief gets frightened or excited and kills the bank teller, even though he hadn't planned to."

"I maintain even that gives the killer a special pleasure, a heightened sensation."

"A sexual sensation?"

"Yes."

"But," said Jack at the end of the table, "the sex urge is a life-giving thing. Murder, obviously, is life-destroying. I don't see how the two can interconnect."

"It's power," said Norton, quietly. "Part of the pleasure of sex is the feeling of power over the partner at the moment of orgasm, the power of inducing pleasure in the partner. And taking another life is exercising the greatest power. That's where I maintain the connection lies."

"Well, *I* don't connect sex with power," exclaimed Marjorie Henderson, rather indignantly.

"But men do," said Sarah Blake. "They like to dominate women and reduce them to sexual objects. Sex is the ultimate triumph of male over female."

"I disagree," said Norton. "The power-feeling flows both ways. Women dominate men sexually—or they *can*."

"But surely," said Helen, who was drawn into the conversation despite herself, "you're talking about a perversion of the original purpose of sex, which was to reproduce. Animals don't feel sensations of power when they mate, and I think, when you're talking about humans feeling sensations of power during sex, you're talking about pretty sick people."

"Perhaps, though I don't particularly like the word 'sick.' Modern civilization is enormously complex, and the emotions of even the simplest members of it are complex too. I don't say that people are consciously aware of power-sensations when they go to bed with someone, any more than I say the average murderer is consciously aware of power when he kills. I *am* saying that emotionally the power-sensation is there. After all, in America today there are relatively few people who think of sex primarily as a form of reproduction. Most Americans think of sex as a form of pleasure."

"Norton, I think your whole thesis is sheer nonsense," said Marjorie Henderson. "You say every human being is capable of murder, and I say that *I'm* one human being who couldn't possibly commit murder. It's utterly outside my character. I don't even like to swat mosquitoes."

"Perhaps you don't know your character as well as you think, Marjorie," replied Norton. "We've had some pretty spectacular examples lately of people experiencing total reversals in character: quiet, docile schoolgirls becoming radicalized and committing terrorist acts. . . ."

"But you're talking about extraordinary circumstances. If I were kidnapped and afraid for my life and subjected to brainwashing or hypnosis or God knows what, then it's true I *might* do something extreme. But I wouldn't be the same person."

"Wouldn't you? Your brain cells would be the same as they were before. Your character, or new facets of it, would be revealed. History is full of dramatic changes in character: St. Paul's conversion on the road to Damascus, for instance. Life is generally full of dramatic changes in character. The college graduate's character is different from when he entered as a freshman. . . ."

"He's more mature. But he's not going out and commit murder."

"If the college taught murder as a respectable or desirable avocation, he might indeed commit murder—though I'll admit that's farfetched. My point is the potential is there, inside us, able to be tapped. At a simple level, I probably could hypnotize you and induce you, through suggestion, to do foolish things you'd never do normally. Now, the cliché is that no hypnotist can force his subject to do anything contrary to his supposed moral character—commit murder, for instance—but I don't believe it. Given the proper circumstances and techniques, any human apparently can be turned into almost anything. As a dramatic example, look at China. The character of an entire nation has been fantastically altered in one generation through techniques of thought manipulation; and what you can do to a nation—a large group of individuals after all—you can certainly do to an individual. I'm afraid the truth we don't like to face is that the old notion of moral character is no longer really applicable. We're not born with any built-in moral fail-safes or taboos. We're born with an infinite capacity to change, to be changed, to be manipulated."

"If that's true," said Marjorie, "we're a very sick world indeed."

"There's that word again. Society is changing. What was 'sick' in 1920 is accepted today. What's 'sick' today may be normal fifty years from now. As a scientist, 'sick' is a word I worry about.''

"Well, I'm sick of this conversation," said Helen, getting up. "And as the hostess, I hereby declare a moratorium on sex *and* violence."

"What will we talk about?" asked Marcia glumly.

"Wine," said Jack, passing the decanter around the table his wife had cleared. But Helen had other ideas. She knew Norton was unusually well read in all fields of science, and after the lamb and asparagus had been served and the Beaune poured, she said, "Norton, did you ever hear of a star called 'Tau Ceti'?"

He looked up, his narrow, dark face a study in surprise.

"I have. But where did *you* hear about it?"

She glanced down the table at Jack, recalling the intensity of Star Child's warning.

"I had a rather strange dream last night," she said. "I can't remember much about it, except it had something to do with a star called 'Tau Ceti,' and I wondered if such a star exists."

"It not only exists," said Norton, "it's a rather special star. It's in the Constellation Cetus, the Whale, which is in the southern hemisphere. Stars are assigned letters of the Greek alphabet coupled with the genitive case of the Latin name for the constellation, so Tau Ceti is 'T' of the Constellation Cetus."

"But why is it special?"

"Because of all the stars that are in the neighborhood, so to speak—Tau Ceti is only twelve light-years from the sun, so it's very close in astronomical terms—it's the one most likely to have a planetary system capable of supporting life."

She almost dropped her fork. "Then you believe in extraterrestrial life?"

"Anyone with any knowledge of astronomy knows there's a probability that life exists somewhere else in the universe. I've even read convincing arguments that the two moons of Mars—Phobos and Deimos—

are actually artificial satellites launched by a Martian civilization millions of years ago before it died out. But forgetting our rather insignificant solar system, there are hundreds of billions of planets in our galaxy revolving around stable suns like our own, and I can't believe that at least some of them haven't developed life. Tau Ceti is a favorite star of people like myself who fantasize about making contact with another civilization because, among other things, Tau Ceti is near us and very much like our sun in size and brilliancy."

"But," said Jack, "if there were a civilization on one of Tau Ceti's planets, could it send some kind of spaceship here?"

Norton spread his thin, hairy hands.

"Who knows? But why not? All right, let's let our imaginations go wild for a moment, helped along by the wine. Let's say a planet revolving around Tau Ceti has a highly advanced technical civilization which, for some reason, decides to send a spacevehicle to us. Now, Tau Ceti is a little over twelve light-years from our sun, which is roughly seventy-six trillion miles. So there are two enormous problems to overcome: the length of time necessary to cover such a huge distance, and the amount of fuel required to propel the ship. Let's take the first problem, time. In order to go seventy-six trillion miles in the lifetime of a crew member—assuming their lifespans are similar to ours—the ship is going to have to go at a relativistic speed, a speed approaching the speed of light, which is about 670 million miles an hour."

"Is it possible to go that fast?" asked Jack.

"Not at the speed of light: nothing with mass can go that fast. But assume they can approach that speed. Now, we know from Einstein that time is diluted as we approach the speed of light. The clock slows down. So if the spaceship were going that fast, while the trip would take twelve years *Earth* time to complete, on the ship itself the time would be much less. Therefore to the space traveler the trip might be a pleasant jaunt of, say, a couple of years. He could sleep a lot, write an autobiographical novel, do crossword puzzles . . ."

"Or watch dirty movies," suggested Marcia Bernstein.

"Exactly. They'd probably equip him with a film library. Now: the second problem, fuel. It's conceivable, even in terms of our own technology, to build a ramjet-type engine that could attain enormous speeds in space. But to do it would require an engine powered by something like controlled thermonuclear fusion."

"What?" interrupted Helen, so loudly that everyone turned to stare at her.

"I said, an engine powered by controlled thermonuclear fusion."

"Then there *is* such a thing?"

"Of course. It's the power of the sun, the primal energy source of the universe."

Her heart was thumping, whether from fear or amazement she wasn't sure. The improbable things she had heard in the improbable dream the night before she was now hearing in reality. Tau Ceti existed. Controlled thermonuclear fusion existed.

Perhaps Star Child existed . . . but that was impossible. . . .

"I think you and Helen had this planned," said Jack, who was looking down the table at his wife with a curious expression.

"Had what planned?" asked Norton.

"This whole conversation. She asked me last night about this Tau Ceti thing, and about controlled thermonuclear fusion . . . what's the game?"

"There's no game," said Norton.

"I must have been reading about this somewhere," lied Helen, "and it got into my dreams."

"You dream about nuclear fusion?" said Marcia disbelievingly. "God, what a bore. I dream about Robert Redford."

The laughter broke the tension, and Helen dropped the subject. But after dinner, when everyone returned to the living room to drink champagne, she took Norton aside and said, "When you say it's the power of the sun, what do you mean exactly?"

He tried as best he could to explain it. He told her that thermonuclear fusion was a branch of plasma physics, plasma being the name science had given to ionized gas. The core of the sun was an enormous mass of hydrogen plasma, or completely ionized hydrogen gas, which was under fantastic pressure—a pressure estimated to be 450 billion atmospheres, one atmosphere being the average pressure of Earth's air at sea level. At this incredible pressure and at a temperature of twenty million degrees, the hydrogen ions underwent fusion—which was, he explained, basically four hydrogen ions combining to produce a single helium ion, helium being the next most complex element after hydrogen. The process of hydrogen fusing into helium released an enormous amount of energy: one *gram* of hydrogen converted to helium releasing an explosive force equivalent to 150 tons of TNT, or 160,000 kilowatt-hours of electrical power. In the sun, the energy was released as heat and light—the sunshine that warmed and illuminated Earth. The sun, then—like all stars in the universe—was a huge thermonuclear fusion furnace which constantly converted hydrogen to helium, every second changing four million tons of matter into energy which it radiated into space. Yet such was the huge size of the sun that, even though it had been doing this for five billion years, it could continue to do so for another five to ten billion years—and at the end of that time, when all the sun's hydrogen was fused into helium, such was the miraculous economy of the process that the helium sun would be only about 1 percent lighter than the original all-hydrogen sun.

"Now," said Norton, "if man could duplicate this process here on Earth—which we're tying to do—not only would we have a literally endless supply of cheap energy—because the oceans are filled with hydrogen—we would also have a nonpolluting source of energy, because the fusion process is almost totally clean, unlike atomic reactors. In fact, atomic power is peanuts compared to fusion power—it's like gas lights compared to a laser. The benefits of fusion power are mind-boggling. For instance, you could toss a used aircraft carrier into the fusion furnace and in seconds it would be reduced to gas. Then you could reclaim all the iron, copper and so forth that had been used to make the carrier and recycle the pure metals. The Earth would never run out of anything. Think of it! Limitless *clean* power, limitless resources which could produce limitless wealth for the whole world . . . It's no wonder scientists are knocking themselves out to design fusion reactors. But the problems are also mind-boggling, because what's involved essentially is recreating a star here on earth. I suppose it's probably the greatest technological challenge man has ever tackled, and when it's solved—*if* it's solved—it will probably bring about the most fundamental change in civilization since . . ."

"Since the harnessing of electricity?" she said, remembering Star Child's comparison.

"Oh, easily that. I think it would be the greatest development since man learned to use fire. It would be like Prometheus stealing fire from the gods, because it *is* the power of the gods, or God. God designed the universe to operate on thermonuclear fusion."

"And when will it be solved?" she asked.

Norton drained his champagne.

"The best guess is in twenty-five to thirty years," he said. "With luck, around the turn of the next century. And now that I've told you what I know about it, which isn't that much, will you kindly tell me why an attractive young French teacher on her second anniversary night would be so interested in thermonuclear fusion?"

"As I said, I read about it, and it must have fascinated me because last night I dreamed about it."

"Oh, it's fascinating all right. It's so fascinating it numbs the imagination—just like this champagne, which I'm going to have one more glass of, then weave home."

He went to the bar, leaving her alone with her thoughts, which were the strangest she'd ever had in her life. She hadn't read about fusion or Tau Ceti: she had *dreamed* about them. And the implications of that were as numbing to her as the implications of the power of the sun.

"And that's the gift I'm bringing your world," Star Child had said. "The technology to achieve controlled thermonuclear fusion power *now*." Not twenty-five years in the future, but *now*. Prometheus stealing fire from the gods. The power of God. Star Child was bringing it to . . . *her*? Helen Bradford?

It had to be a wild coincidence, a bizarre nightmare, a strange dream. It couldn't be really happening.

But what if—and the thought again filled her with coldest apprehension—what if it *were* happening?

2

Over the top of Rock Mountain from the Bradfords, placed untypically on the north slope, was another Colonial farmhouse dating from the late eighteenth century; and at approximately the time Helen's guests were drinking champagne in her living room, in the attic of the Scovill farmhouse the murderer of Judy Siebert was inspecting himself in a mirror.

Ben Scovill hadn't particularly minded when his father had died the previous May. They had never been close, and Ben liked the idea of being his own master; independence meant a great deal to him. Fascinated by his good looks—more than a little in love with himself—he had long day-dreamed of getting out of Shandy and taking off for Hollywood to try and get into television, or even the movies. He had graduated from Shandy Prep that June. Because his grades had been high and he had an excellent athletic record, he had had his pick of colleges. Ben, however, didn't want to go to college, and his father's death had released him from that burden. He had sold off the herd of Holsteins that had supported the farm, banked the twenty thousand dollars insurance his father had left him, and begun to sell the farm equipment. Aware that soaring land prices had made his hundred rocky acres worth a good deal of money, he had decided to sell the farm as well. The money, the freedom—they were intoxicating.

And then he had begun having the dreams, and his plans were changed.

Now he was standing in front of the mirror in the attic, checking the reflection of his costume against the photograph of Douglas Fairbanks Senior in the book of old movie posters. The movie was *The Thief of Baghdad,* and Fairbanks was frozen in a mid-air leap, wearing a pair of baggy harem trousers and swinging wide a scimitar. Ben was wearing a reasonable facsimile. He had crudely sewn the harem trousers out of an old sheet, and the red sash at his waist had once been a scarf. His sword wasn't a scimitar, but rather a Japanese officer's sword his father had stolen from a lieutenant he had killed in the Second World War and which had lain in an attic trunk ever since. Ben had salvaged it and sharpened the blade. Now he tossed the movie-poster book on the floor and waved the sword around his head.

"Ten thousand lives for the Emperor! Remember Hiroshima! Banzai, banzai!" Then he lowered the sword and declared to the mirror, in a deep voice, "The cameras are ready, Mr. Fairbanks. In this scene, you leap from the walls of the caliph's palace and escape certain death at the hands of his torturers."

He laughed, put the sword on a dusty chair and examined the reflection of his trousers from both sides. Satisfied with his handiwork, he started to leave the mirror when the reflection of his face caught his attention. He looked at himself, running his hands lightly over his bare, hairless chest as he did so. He reached out and put his hands on the mirror, touching the reflection of his chest. He smiled slightly. Stepping up to the mirror, he placed his mouth on the cold glass and kissed his reflection.

He picked up the sword and left the attic, turning out the light and closing the door. He hurried down the narrow, tilted stairs to the second-floor hallway of the ancient farmhouse. Three bedrooms and a small bath opened onto the hall; Ben had taken over the largest bedroom when his father died. It was a pleasant corner room, facing north and east, with faded rose wallpaper his mother had put up twenty years before. There was a black Victorian bureau with an oval mirror that had been in the family for four generations and which Ben suspected was worth some money. A big matching bed, unmade, and two granny rockers were the rest of the original furnishings, but Ben had moved in his steel desk, which was piled with magazines. He had also tacked up numerous Personality Posters of his cult heros: Brando, James Dean, Peter Fonda, Alice Cooper, Guru Maharaj Ji, Jobriath, Stevie Wonder, Bette Midler. On a table was a cheap hi-fi and hundreds of rock albums. Above it, a bookshelf was piled with paperbacks: mysteries by the dozen, science fiction, *Jonathan Livingston Seagull*. The floor was strewn with dirty clothes, more magazines and newspapers. He had been fairly neat when his father had been alive; now he had become a pig and he loved it. Freedom.

He put the sword on the desk and flopped back down on the bed, lay there a while lazily scratching his bare stomach, once pushing his hand into his homemade harem trousers to fondle his genitals.

But he wasn't interested in masturbation now: he had other things on his mind. He sat up and looked at the electric clock on his desk: nine thirty. Then he leaned down and picked up one of the newspapers on the floor. It was the *Sunday Fairfax Bulletin,* the only newspaper in the county. He opened it to the third page and looked again at the article he had circled that morning. The headline read, "Realtor Goes to Convention." The gist of the article was that Mr. Arnold Fredericks of 225 Hudson Street, Fairfax, had left the previous day for Washington, D.C., to attend a national realtors' convention, and that he wouldn't be back till the following Tuesday. His wife Betty was staying home to take care of their ten-month-old son Anthony.

He ran his finger under the address, fixing it in his mind. Then he got up to dress himself. Ten minutes later he turned out all the lights and let himself out the front door. The house, well set back from Rock Mountain Road, was in fairly bad shape: its white paint was peeling (a condition that wasn't helped by the northern exposure), the roofline sagged, the top of its chimney was missing a dozen bricks. The twelve-on-twelve eyes of the place had cataracts: cheap plastic storm windows Ben had been too lazy to take off that summer. No matter. The house might be something of a derelict, but Ben thought it would be standing a hundred years from now—something he wouldn't say for most of the modern houses he saw.

He left the front porch and walked to the red barn, where he got in his father's 1969 green Dodge. Starting the car, he drove down the drive to Rock Mountain Road, then headed north for Fairfax, twelve miles away. He knew where Hudson Street was, and twenty minutes later he was parked across the street from 225.

It was a quiet block with one street light at the end; 225 was the third house in. It was an unpretentious place with white aluminum siding and bright green shutters. Set on a small lot, its driveway went in next to the kitchen and a tall lilac hedge served as a screen from the house next door, which he noticed was dark. Across the street was an empty field.

It couldn't be better.

Satisfied, Ben shifted into Drive and pulled away from the curb to return home.

When Norman Akroyd, Sarah Blake, the Hendersons and the Bernsteins finally left the party at eleven, Helen Bradford closed the front door and turned on her husband, who was slumped in a chair in front of the fireplace.

"*You* got drunk!" she snapped.

"Fuck you," he said. In fact, Jack Bradford was well on his way to alcoholic oblivion. His eyes were half-closed, his coat was off, he held an empty champagne glass in his hand, and there was a sullen expression on his face. After the martinis and wine at dinner, the post-prandial champagne had indeed done him in.

Helen started cleaning ashtrays.

"We can skip the four-letter bit," she said. "I'd think on our anniversary you could manage to stay sober—particularly with the Hendersons here. Lyman's a good sport and all that, but he doesn't like to see his faculty stumble-down drunk."

"Fuck Lyman Henderson."

"Oh, *stop* it. God, I hate you when you get drunk. And you were a little obvious with Marcia."

He sat up and tried to focus his eyes on her.

"And what does that mean?"

"You know. You kept looking at her all evening as if you wanted to take her out to the barn."

"We don't have a barn."

"That doesn't matter. Marcia would do it in a tree."

"What about you and Norton?"

"Oh, come on."

"What's this little game you two are up to? Tau Shitty, or whatever the hell the name is. Thermofusion nuclear. What's going on between you two?"

"Jack, that's crazy. Norton's one of our dearest friends—you know he'd never try anything . . ."

"Norton's *sick*," he said, pointing a finger at her. "Sick. All that shit about murder and sex: that's sick stuff. You'd better watch out, or lover-boy'll slit your throat to get his rocks off."

He slumped back in the chair as she glared at him.

"You're drunk," she stated, scornfully.

"What was the dream you had?" he asked, staring at the empty fireplace.

"I told you I don't remember."

"Don't lie to me. You remember. What was it?"

She continued cleaning the room.

"I'm going to bed," she said, "and I suggest you do the same before you pass out."

He sat up and hurled the champagne glass across the room at her. It narrowly missed her hair and shattered against the white-paneled wall.

"What *is* it?"

She was trembling.

"Jack . . ."

"You've been dreaming about Raymond, haven't you?" he said. "Tell me the truth, goddam it! What'd he say to you?"

"What did *who* say—?"

"RAYMOND!"

Suddenly, he leaned over and buried his face in his hands. Alarmed, she set down the paper bag she'd been dumping cigarette stubs in and hurried to his side. Kneeling beside him, she put her arms around him.

"Jack, what is it?" she said. "What's wrong?"

He looked up at her, his bloodshot eyes streaming tears.

"I'm afraid."

"Of *what?*"

He started to say something, then changed his mind. Pushing her arms away, he got to his feet and stumbled across the flokati rug toward the stairs.

"Jack, what are you afraid of?"

He didn't answer until he had reached the stairs. Then, stopping at the bottom and leaning on the rail, he turned to look at her. She couldn't tell whether his expression was one of confusion or hostility. He said one word:

"Raymond."

Then he started up the stairs. She ran across the room.

"But who in God's name is Raymond?" she called.

He didn't answer. By the time she had turned out

48

the lights and joined him upstairs, he had passed out on the bed.

By the time she woke up the next morning, he was gone.

He was frightened and confused and, at the same time, intrigued. He was also hungover. When he woke up, he didn't remember much of the shank of the previous evening, but he remembered getting drunk and he didn't want another lecture from Helen. He got out of bed, put on his clothes and tiptoed down the stairs out of the house. He climbed in his mustard-colored Volvo and drove down the mountain to the deserted campus. He wanted to be alone to think, to try and understand what was happening to him. He also wanted to take a swim to revitalize his hungover body.

He parked in front of the modern gym, got out of his car and saw Ben Scovill's green Dodge in front of the building. So Ben must have decided to work out a little. Despite his need for solitude, the idea of seeing Ben pleased him. Going into the empty locker room, he stripped, put on his bathing suit and headed for the indoor pool. It had been donated by a millionaire alumnus and was an Olympic-sized beauty. As he approached the pool area, he heard the sound of someone jumping up and down on the diving board. That would be Ben. When he went into the big room, he saw him poised at the end of the high board.

"Good morning," said Ben, and Jack looked at his young former pupil. As always, he took a certain esthetic pleasure in seeing Ben's well-made body, though sometimes he somewhat nervously asked himself if the pleasure were something other than esthetic.

Ben turned around and stood backward at the end of the board.

"A back double gainer," he announced, "in the tuck position."

He sprang off the board, arching backward into the air like an inverted bird. Then, tucking himself in a ball, he twirled twice before straightening to slice into the turquoise water.

"How was that?" he called as he surfaced.

"Not bad," said Jack. In fact, it had been beautifully executed.

"Your turn, coach."

"Not this morning, thanks," Jack said as he dived off the side of the pool. He felt a pleasant shock as he hit the water and submerged. Then he surfaced a few feet away from Ben, who was treading water.

"You've stayed in practice," said Jack.

"I come down every once in a while."

"That's good."

He relaxed on his back and floated aimlessly.

"What's the latest on Judy Siebert?" asked Ben.

"Still missing."

"I hear the State Police think she ran away."

"Could be."

"What if I told you I knew where she was?"

Jack stopped floating. Treading water, he looked at Ben, whose face showed a slight grin.

"Where?"

"At my house."

"You mean she's been with you since Wednesday night?"

"That's right."

"Well, God, Ben, why didn't you tell someone? Her father's really shook up. . . ."

"So what?"

Jack wondered what was going on. Ben seemed to be toying with him, and enjoying it. . . .

"Would you like to see her?"

"Not particularly."

"I *want* you to see her, Mr. Bradford."

The soft slapping of the wavelets against the sides of the pool was the only sound in the cavernous room.

"What's going on, Ben?" he asked quietly.

"Come up to my house and I'll show you." He abruptly dived beneath the surface and frogged his way underwater to the side of the pool. Then he hoisted himself out and looked back at Jack. Again he grinned as he said, "I knew you were going to be here this morning."

"How did you know?"

"Raymond told me."

With that, he walked out of the pool area into the locker room.

Even without Ben's cryptic remark and his sphingine silence while they got dressed, Jack would have known something strange was happening. Ben was trying to conceal his excitement, but it escaped from him like sweat—and, like sweat, Jack could almost smell it. How did *Ben* know about Raymond? How did "Raymond" know he was going to the gym that morning when even *he* didn't know until he had awakened? It was as if there were a third presence in the locker room, an invisible person or thing whose identity Ben knew and Jack was beginning to suspect.

He followed Ben's Dodge up the mountain past his house into the drive of the ancient farmhouse, which squatted on the north slope like a wart. Silently he followed Ben to the porch and into the living room. Then he said, "Where is she?"

"In the cellar."

They went into the littered kitchen, where Ben walked to the corner and pulled open a trapdoor.

"Come on."

He turned on the light and started down the steps. Jack followed. When he reached the dirt floor, Ben was standing in the middle of the room beside the clean cot, which had been shoved against the stone wall. Directly above his head was the ceiling bulb that spilled light down his face, creating an eerie chiaroscuro.

"Well?" said Jack, looking around.

51

Ben pointed to the ground under his feet.

"She's down there," he said simply. "I sacrificed her to Raymond."

Jack Bradford's first instinct was to run out of the house: there was terror in that ancient cellar. Not only the terror of violent death, but the terror of the dreams that had been ripping his mind apart the past few nights. The thing that had appeared in his mind, the thing that called itself Raymond and claimed it was the new God, the thing that insinuated evil obscenities into his unconsciousness, driving him near the point of total despair . . . Now, suddenly, he was face to face with it in Ben Scovill's cellar. Or rather, he was face to face with Ben, who claimed he, too, knew Raymond. . . . He wanted to run but he couldn't. He was rooted by curiosity, and intrigued—for he had to admit to himself that many of the things Raymond had whispered were not new thoughts in his mind, but ideas that had lain submerged. He had even wondered if Raymond were a manifestation of his own alter-ego, or the beginnings of schizophrenia. But how could that be, if Ben had seen Raymond too? Unless there was some other rational explanation he hadn't thought of . . .

"You know who Raymond is?" he said uncertainly.

"Of course. And so do you. He told me you did."

"But I *don't* know who he is! Or *what* he is . . ."

"He's a god," said Ben matter-of-factly. "He says he is, and what else could he be? Who else but a god could come inside your mind like that, night after night? It's a miracle . . ."

"I don't believe in miracles."

"You *have* to, Jack, it's happening, and we're in on it! It's a new age, second coming, whatever you want to call it. The Master says the world needs a new god, and it's true. It's time for Raymond."

"But why did you kill Judy Siebert—if you did?"

"It was a love-death, and it was beautiful, just like Raymond said it would be."

His youthful, unlined face was damn near radiant, and Jack Bradford felt bilious.

"Christ, Ben, that's crazy . . ."

"It's not crazy, it's beautiful. You want to try it, don't you?" He came closer to him and put his hand on Jack's upper arm. "Raymond wants you to do it, but *you* want to. It's a sacrifice to him, an act of love. It's the most exciting, satisfying thing I've ever experienced."

Jack felt Ben rubbing his arm slowly, and he panicked. The physical attraction he had at times vaguely felt for the younger man was now being induced by Ben himself, as if his metamorphosis included becoming an aggressive bisexual, something Jack had never sensed in him before. That terrified Jack as much as the crazy idea of a love-death. He pushed Ben's hand off.

"I don't believe you killed anyone. This is a goddam put-on."

"No it's not . . ."

"Then it's Norton Akroyd. He's put all this sick shit in your head . . . 'the joy of murder.' . . ."

"It's Raymond, you know that!"

"No, I *don't* know it," said Jack, backing away from him. "It's got to be Norton. He's managed to hypnotize us somehow . . . Christ, he must be doing it to Helen too. . . ."

"Come *on,* Jack. He's not hypnotizing anyone—that's stupid."

"Don't call me 'Jack,' dammit," he shouted. "I'm Mr. Bradford."

"You're my brother," Ben said softly, holding out both hands toward the older man. "Raymond wants us both to be his apostles. . . ."

He was at the stairs now, and he didn't want to hear any more. He took one last, half-angry, half-frightened look at Ben, then ran up the wooden steps and out of the house.

*　　*　　*

Norton Akroyd slammed a serve across the net to Lyman Henderson, who maneuvered his adipose body with surprising agility and managed to return the ball with a high lob. It sailed over the tennis court as Norton backed up, shielding his eyes from the sun with his free hand to try and spot the fuzzy white sphere.

"Out!" he yelled as the ball bonked on the clay an inch over the line.

"Damn," growled the headmaster, wiping the sweat from his face. Lyman's one sport was tennis, which he loved with a passion, even though his addiction never did seem to achieve for him the hoped-for loss of weight. As Norton retrieved the ball, he saw Jack Bradford's Volvo pull up beside the court. Jack leapt out of the car and ran across the short stretch of lawn that separated the court from the campus road, then onto the court itself.

"What are you doing to me?" he yelled almost manically, charging up to Norton.

"Huh?"

"You heard me." He was panting from exertion and anger. "First it was Helen, now it's Ben Scovill . . . what's this goddam game you're playing? Are you trying to prove your stupid theories about murder and sex?"

"Jack, I have no idea what you're talking about. . . ."

"Yes you do." He grabbed Norton's white Lacoste tennis shirt with his left hand and jerked the slender psychiatrist toward him till their noses were almost touching. "Listen, Norton, I don't understand what you're doing to my head or how you're doing it. And I don't understand how the hell you've got Ben and Helen in on the put-on. But, if you don't stop it, I'm going to the police. Understand?"

Lyman Henderson had hurried around the net, a worried look on his round, red face.

"Jack, what's the matter?"

Jack released a frightened Norton and turned to the headmaster.

"Norton's been zapping my mind—somehow," he snapped. "I don't know if it's hypnosis or what the hell it is, but it's going to stop. *Now*." He looked back at Norton. "I mean it, I'll go to the goddam police."

He walked away from the two tennis players, who, in an apparent state of shock, watched him return to his Volvo.

"Is he still drunk?" said Lyman in a muted voice.

"No, he's sober," replied Norton.

"Then what's he talking about?"

Norton's answer sounded as confused as his face looked.

"I have no idea."

"Where've you been?" asked Helen ten minutes later as her husband came in the living room of the house. He didn't answer. Rather, he walked over to her. She was sitting on the white flokati rug surrounded by the *Times*.

"You know," he said, "I've been fairly honest with you. Now I want you to be honest with me."

"About what?"

"About what you and Ben and Norton are up to, and about Raymond. The things Norton was talking about last night seem to be happening. Maybe he's trying out his theories on me by hypnotic suggestion . . . something. . . . However or whatever . . . I just warned him to stop, and now I'm warning *you*. No more of this Raymond business. Understand?"

"Jack, I told you last night I have *no* idea who Raymond is! If I knew, I'd tell you because I know for some reason he's frightening you. . . ."

"Then you didn't have a dream the other night. That was a lie."

She got to her feet. "No, it wasn't!"

"Why did Norton tell you to pretend you dreamed about some stupid star?"

"He didn't tell me anything! I *did* have a dream—it was weird and frightening. . . ."

"Then what was it about?"

She closed her eyes tight, frustrated, on the verge of tears.

"I can't tell you."

"Why?"

She opened her eyes and looked at him defiantly.

"Because you wouldn't believe me if I did, and because I've sworn not to."

"Sworn? To whom? Norton?"

"No, for God's sake, Norton has nothing to *do* with it. I swore to . . . Star Child."

He blinked. "Star Child? Who's *he?*"

She gave up. She sank into the sofa in front of the fireplace and sighed.

"All right, since *not* telling you is going to have us at each other's throats, I'll tell you. I had this extremely realistic dream in which a young boy who calls himself Star Child and claims he comes from a planet of the star Tau Ceti told me he's bringing to Earth the secret of controlled thermonuclear fusion. Now, I'm perfectly aware that sounds absolutely nutty as all hell, but Jack, I had never heard of Tau Ceti, and I'd never heard of thermonuclear fusion, so how could I possibly have dreamed about them? I mean, you can't dream things that aren't already somewhere in your mind, can you?"

He was frowning. His initial look of incredulity was being replaced by something else. Rather to her surprise, she thought he actually did believe her.

"Do you swear to me that's true?"

"Yes. Jack, I love you, and I hated not telling you but this Star Child was so adamant that I not tell . . ."

"Then Norton *didn't* have anything to do with it?"

"Not as far as I know. I'd guess it was coincidence that he mentioned thermonuclear fusion last night, and believe me, I was amazed to find out there is such a thing. Amazed, and . . . and frightened."

"Why?"

"Well, if the dream is for *real*—then this Star Child or whatever it is must be coming here as he said . . ."

"Then . . ." He thought a moment. ". . . then Raymond, wherever, whatever he is, must be coming, too."

"Would someone tell me who Raymond is? Star Child's weird enough, but who is Raymond?"

He didn't answer. He was looking past her, staring at the bookcase, lost in thought.

"Who *is* he?" she repeated insistently.

He focused his attention back on her.

"Raymond must be what he claims he is . . ."

He smiled slightly, shook his head, stuck his hands in his pockets and went into the kitchen to get a beer. Despite all her pleading, cajoling and even threats, he refused to discuss the subject further. He spent the rest of the day working on the compost heap, and she finally gave up trying to elicit more information about Raymond. That night they went to a country inn for dinner and ate in near-total silence. He was not hostile—merely uncommunicative. She knew he was brooding about something (Raymond?). He had no cocktails and only two glasses of wine during the meal, scoring a near-record on the Jack Bradford Abstinence Scale. Then they went home to bed. He said he was too tired to make love, which annoyed her even though in her distraught state she wasn't feeling especially amorous.

They turned out the lights, turned their backs to each other, and then . . . silence. As she listened to his barely audible breathing behind her, she wondered what was happening to her marriage and her life.

3

At nine o'clock that night, a hot and tired Betty Fredericks of 225 Hudson Street, Fairfax, sat down in front of the Zenith set in her small living room to watch a rerun of "Masterpiece Theatre." Her ten-month-old son, Anthony, had finally gone to sleep, though he had been in a rotten mood and had been wailing ever since she put him to bed. But now, at last, silence from the bedroom off the living room. Betty had made herself an iced coffee; the reception on Channel Thirteen was better than usual. The attractive, thirty-two-year-old brunette could relax.

It was then she heard the car pull into her driveway.

Since she was alone with Anthony, the unexpected visitor rather alarmed her. Getting out of her husband's Barcalounger chair, she went into the kitchen, turned on the light, then went to the back door to look out. It was a green Dodge and, as she turned on the outside light, she saw a nice-looking man get out. He was neatly dressed, and though she couldn't understand why he had driven to the end of the drive and parked in front of the garage instead of parking on the street, her alarm subsided.

The sound of the car, however, had awakened Anthony, who had begun to wail again. Damn, she thought, as she unlocked the door and opened it.

"Yes?" The young man had come to the back stoop. She left the screen door locked.

"Is Mr. Fredericks in?"

"Not just now. Could I help you? I'm Mrs. Fredericks."

"Oh. Well, you see I just inherited a farm down in Shandy, and I was thinking of putting it on the market. I know your husband's in real estate and I thought he'd be interested. When will he be back?"

"He was supposed to be here Tuesday, but he called today and said he's flying into Hartford tomorrow morning. Why don't you leave your name and number, and I'll have him call you?"

"That'll be fine."

She unhooked the screen door and let him in the kitchen.

"Sorry to bother you this late."

"Oh, that's all right. I'll get a pad and pencil. . . ."

She went to the kitchen table and opened the drawer as Anthony's cries escalated.

"That your baby?" asked Ben.

"Yes. He's in one of his moods tonight. I think it's the heat."

"Don't you get a little nervous here all alone with him?"

She turned, holding a legal pad and a pencil.

"Oh, a little. But Fairfax isn't exactly Crime City, is it? Now, if you'll put your name here . . ."

His right fist smashed into her nose. Shafts of light bit her retinas as the fist hit her chin. Grunting, she fell back on the steel-topped table. Then she collapsed on the linoleum floor.

He pulled two pieces of clothesline from his pocket, straddled her, turned her over on her stomach, jerked her wrists together behind her back and quickly tied them. Then her ankles. Next, he pulled a white linen napkin from his other pocket, twirled it into a gag, and forced it into her mouth, tying it tight behind her head. Then he stood up and turned all the lights out, including the living room. Now the house was dark except for the ghostly glow of "Masterpiece Theatre." From the bedroom, Anthony's sobs mingled with the cultivated tones of Alistair Cooke.

He picked her up and hoisted her over his shoulder like a sack of flour. Going to the screen door, he pushed it open and left the house, leaving the kitchen door ajar. He hurried across the dark back lawn to his car, opened the back door with difficulty, and then dumped her in, head-first. She sprawled on the back seat, her head dangling. He pushed her off the seat onto the floor, then closed the door. Quickly looking at the house next door, which was still dark, he got into the front seat and started the car. He backed down the driveway to the street and checked both directions. Nothing.

Backing onto the street, he turned the car and started for Shandy. He left his lights off until he had turned the corner of Hudson Street.

Helen found herself in the Beautiful Valley again.

As before, the sun was shining in a cloudless sky, sparkling off the stream in a billion shards of fire. Ahead of her was the apple tree. Beneath it stood Star Child. She went toward him, becoming aware that again she was wearing the flowing white robe.

As she came near Star Child, she saw he looked angry.

"You told your husband," he said as she seated herself on the rock. "You betrayed my trust."

"How do you know?"

"I'm in your mind. I know your thoughts."

"Then you should know I had to tell him. Something strange is happening to him, something I don't understand."

"Raymond," he interrupted.

"Who *is* he?"

"He's very dangerous. He knows the techniques of thought projection, and he's sending his mind into your peoples', calling himself a god. He's no more a god—or a devil—than I am, but he is dangerous, and he can make your husband dangerous."

"Dangerous?" she asked. "To whom?"

"To you. Thought projection can be used to dominate a mind. It can turn a mind inside out. It can make a healthy mind sick, and a sick mind insane."

"But why should he do such a thing?"

"It must be that he wants your husband to destroy you so that you can't help me."

As he spoke, a strong wind suddenly sprang up which began whipping the branches of the apple tree. Dark clouds appeared out of nowhere and began scuttling across the sun. Star Child looked at the sky.

"It's *him*," he said. "I thought he might try this . . ."

"Try what?"

"Thought-project into your mind. Raymond," he called at the top of his voice, trying to be heard over the wind, which was now almost a roar, "Raymond, you son of a bitch, what do you want? What are you trying to do?"

There was a flash of light and a clap of thunder. She put her hands over her eyes. When she looked again, Star Child had vanished. In the place he had been standing in coiled a hissing rattlesnake.

Edging her way around the rock she had been sitting on, she began running away from the tree toward the stream. By now the valley was dark, and it had begun to rain. Sheets of water, whipped by the blasting wind, beat into her face as she stumbled down the short embankment to the stream.

Suddenly, she found herself floating in a void, twisting lazily in a yellow-orange vacuum.

Then she was standing in a dark cemetery.

All was silent. She looked down at the white robe she was wearing. A moment before, it had been soaked. Now it was dry, as was she, and a lazy breeze puffed it slightly, coiling it around her body like a pillar of smoke.

She looked around her. Although the night sky was black, somehow she could see the tilted Colonial tombstones girdled with weeds. Ahead of her stood a limestone mausoleum, its heavy bronze doors guarded by two Victorian funerary statues of kneeling, mourning angels. Above the door, where the family name would normally be chiseled, was a blank stone.

She was frightened. She told herself that somehow the thing, person or whatever called Raymond had invaded her sleeping mind, somehow expelling Star Child in the process, that this was all a magic-lantern show, stage tricks calculated to mold her will through fright to whatever purpose Raymond might have. The knowledge that it was trickery made it none the less disturbing. The dream-reality was as vivid as waking reality. She felt vague, primordial nibblings of ghost-fear.

And then the bronze doors of the mausoleum started slowly to open, the heavy metal grating on the hinges. She tried to run but found her feet weighted with lead. A figure appeared in the door of the tomb. It was wrapped in a phosphorescent shroud that glowed. Its hand held a white mask over its face which entirely concealed the features, two eye-slits alone piercing the screen. A tomblike voice came from behind the mask, saying, "I am Raymond, the son of Starfire, the one and only god. Worship me or be destroyed."

It was Gothic, childish, in a way almost ridiculous. Yet she felt herself riveted with fear. If it was nothing but a magic-lantern show, nevertheless she was *in* it. No, it was more like being in a movie . . . a kind of slick Hammer Films horror production that had somehow weirdly come to life and was starring *her*.

She forced herself to challenge.

"You're a bluff . . . you're not a god and you don't frighten me . . ."

The figure remained immobile for a moment, then moved out of the doorway of the mausoleum and started toward her. Its silence seemed even more menacing. She tried to back away from it but found her feet still couldn't move.

"Who *are* you?" she said. "Why are you putting on this absurd spook-show? I'm not some six-year-old you can scare with bad dreams."

By now the figure was standing less than three feet in front of her, and she became aware of a stench, sickening-sweet, loathsome. It stopped and lowered its mask. The face was her husband's. It was stoney, and its eyes intense with what seemed to her a crazed look. Suddenly, with dramatic swiftness, his hands grabbed the front of his shroud, and he opened the garment wide, like a Central Park flasher, holding it outward like an extended opera cape. She looked down at his body, which was naked. It was in the last stages of decomposition. Crawling over the green-black flesh were maggots, worms and roaches. In places they had stripped the flesh away, exposing the skeleton; the genitalia were partly destroyed. The whole sight was so repulsive she felt her stomach convulse with nausea. She sank to her knees, and turned her face away to vomit.

"Go away," she whimpered. "Please. Go away."

Silence.

She slowly turned her face back toward the apparition.

She was alone in the graveyard.

Unsteadily, she got to her feet and looked at the mausoleum. The doors were closed. Above them, on the stone lintel that had previously been blank, was now carved in bas-relief a single word:

BRADFORD.

She woke up.

She was shivering. Her head was, again, splitting. She turned to look at her husband, who was gone. She sat up and turned on the bed light.

"Jack?" she called softly.

Silence.

She got out of bed, put on a bathrobe and hurried

out of the room. In the hall she could see a light was on downstairs. She descended to the living room, where she saw Jack sitting in the chair before the fireplace. He had put on his plaid bathrobe and was smoking a cigarette, which he rarely did. His hairy legs extended from beneath the bathrobe, and his bare feet were crossed casually in the long white wool of the flokati rug.

She started across the room, saying, "I dreamed about Raymond."

He watched her, but said nothing. She stopped by his chair.

"Do you suppose you were right? Do you think Norton *is* hypnotizing us—coming into our dreams as either Star Child or Raymond?"

Silence.

"Star Child called it 'thought projection.' Do you think Norton could have learned how to project his thoughts into other people's dreams?"

Finally he spoke:

"What in *hell* are you talking about?"

"Raymond. I just dreamt about him, and he's disgusting! And I'm admitting maybe you were right about Norton trying to prove his theories by manipulating our minds. Star Child told me thought projection can make a sane mind mad, which is almost the same thing Norton was saying . . ." She stopped. Something was wrong. She said dryly, "You *do* remember Raymond?"

"I remember hearing you say his name in your sleep."

"Your memory seems curiously adaptable. Don't you remember last night? You were talking about being so terrified of him. . . ."

"Last night I was drunk."

"You weren't drunk this morning. Jack, don't play *games* with me. Something weird, maybe dangerous is happening to both of us. . . ."

"Then why don't you go see Norton?"

"He may be involved in it. You said so yourself."

"Come on, I was putting you on. Who do you think Norton is, Svengali? He goes around shooting out thought rays, turning people into zombies?"

"But that was *your* idea."

"Well I suspect it was a gin-soaked one. The point is, if you're being bothered by strange dreams, go see a psychiatrist, Norton—he's the dream maven."

"But you're having the dreams too. You *told* me."

"Did I?" His voice was cool as he looked up at her, flicking the ash of his cigarette in a crystal ashtray. "You know, Helen, the mind is a delicate thing. Once it starts going, well, out of whack . . ."

"I am *not* going 'out of whack'!"

"Then what do you call it? Indigestion?"

She forced herself to calm down.

"All right," she said, after a moment, "maybe something is wrong with me. And I will see Norton, who may or may not have anything to do with it. But don't pretend nothing's happening with *you*, Jack. Because if I'm going bananas, darling, so are you."

His eyes seemed to bore into hers for a moment, and she remembered the figure in the graveyard, the figure with the face of her husband and the body of a corpse. Death. Her husband was death? Was *that* what the dream had meant?

Saying nothing more to her husband, she walked back across the room and started up the stairs.

Her mind was numb.

4

Douglas Fairbanks looked at the bound woman and his eyes sparkled through the slits of his black half-mask.

"You are the beautiful Princess Fatima, and I have captured you from the palace of your father, the Caliph." He swung the Japanese sword around his head.

Betty Fredericks stared up at the young man in the bizarre outfit and wondered if this could possibly be happening to her, if she were really going to die. It seemed incredible, being spread-eagled on a cot in the middle of a cellar in Shandy, hands and wrists tied to the four corners of the bed while this pleasant-looking man danced around her, dressed in home-made harem pants and a mask. . . . She told herself it had to be some grotesque nightmare. And the weird altar at the end of the room where he had just finished mouthing a prayer to someone named Raymond. . . . Don't panic, she thought, he really won't do it. It's just some crazy game or something. Don't *panic* . . .

Now he put the sword on the dirt floor and leaned over her, his face no more than inches above hers.

"Don't be afraid," he said. "You are part of a beautiful new religion that is coming to our world. Don't be afraid."

"You see," he continued as he unbuttoned the front of her housedress, "the new god has told us to be creative in our worship, to act out our fantasies. I've always wanted to be a kind of swashbuckler like Tony Curtis used to be, and Douglas Fairbanks in the old silents, so I decided we'd try *The Thief of Baghdad*. You're the Princess Fatima. Wouldn't your rather be a princess for one night than a housewife all your life?"

She shook her head.

"But that's the way it's to be, Princess. And now that I've captured you, we'll enjoy a night of love. I'll sing you songs and cover your body with my kisses."

He ripped open the rest of her dress and tore at her panties. Her vulva was now exposed.

"Princess, you're beautiful to behold." He leaned over and placed his mouth in her pubic hairs.

His penis was throbbing now. The chapel of Raymond . . . How true it was, he thought. As Raymond said, how much more satisfying *this* way . . .

He untied the red scarf-sash. His penis arched upward like a scimitar. He put himself inside her, shoving deeper and deeper against her tightness.

She had always been terrified by the idea of rape. Now that it was happening, she found the terror worse than her imaginings. The myth that rape-victims secretly enjoyed it was, she was finding by experience, totally untrue. How could she or anybody enjoy having her body invaded by a maniac? This *religious* maniac . . . What was the religion? His own, something he made up? Oh God . . . terror made her whole body ache.

"My Princess," he repeated, as he reached climax.

She heard him actually start to pray, or so it sounded. Something about Raymond, the one and only god that he had consecrated his life to, who taught him a special delight and ecstasy.

Now he had climbed off her and stood beside the cot, looking down at her face.

He leaned over and kissed her on the forehead.

"Now you will live with Raymond," he said.

He stepped back and picked up the Japanese sword.

She turned her face away, her eyes now blank. He raised the sword above his head, aimed, brought it down with all his strength.

He had carefully sharpened the blade, yet it took two strokes to sever the neck from the trunk.

PART II

The Acts
of the Apostles

1

The school's small psychology building was set, without a hint of self-consciousness, next to the handsome Georgian chapel. Beline Hall, named after the alumnus who had provided the funds, was a plain rectangular brick building containing a lecture hall, two laboratories, four small classrooms and a consulting suite consisting of Norton Akroyd's office space and two small rooms in which he could treat those students seeking psychiatric care. The next morning at ten, Helen seated herself in front of her friend's desk and said, "Norton, I realize this is a weird question to start off the day with, but . . . are you working some kind of hypnosis on Jack and me?"

He stared at her for a moment, then shook his head slowly.

"What in God's name *is* this? Yesterday, Jack practically attacked me on the tennis court, and now *you* . . . What makes you think I'm hypnotizing you?"

"The other night at dinner you were saying you could manipulate people's minds by hypnosis. . . ."

"I didn't say that. I said it was possible under certain circumstances to alter or reveal hidden facets of people's characters, but I was only speaking in generalities. I'm certainly not trying to *do* it to Jack or you or anybody. In the first place, I haven't even hypnotized you——"

71

"Then how do you explain the dreams?"

"What dreams?"

She told him about Star Child and Raymond, and he listened, apparently with increasing wonderment. When she finished, he digested what she had said. Then: "I can see why Jack thinks I'm behind it. He must be looking for some rational explanation of what's happening, though I'm not sure how rational it is to say I'm 'zapping' him."

"You have to admit it's a strange coincidence that the very thing you were talking about seems to be happening——"

"But I'm *not* hypnotizing you," he interrupted. "And I certainly don't know how to project my thoughts into other people's dreams. Good God, if I did I certainly wouldn't be stuck here in Shandy."

"Then what's happening to us?"

"I don't know—yet." He paused, collecting his thoughts. Then: "You say Jack's denying the dreams now?"

"Yes, and that worries me more than anything else. Or I should say, frightens me. He's starting to play a game with me, and I don't know what's really going on in his head. . . ." She gestured nervously with her fine-boned hands. "It's all so bizarre. I don't know what's real, whether this Star Child is just a dream but meaning something . . . and God knows what Raymond is supposed to be . . ."

"For the time being let's concentrate on you and leave Jack out of it."

"But the dreams must be interconnected . . ."

"I know, but bear with me. I'm trying to do everything I can to help. You know that. Except we're going to have to be totally honest with each other."

She calmed down. "I know."

"How would you rate your marriage? Any strains developed recently?"

She shrugged. "Well, Jack's been boozing more heavily than usual."

"I noticed that at your party."

"It would have been hard not to. Otherwise, things have been . . . at least I *thought* things were going along well. *I* was happy . . ."

"How about the physical side?"

"It used to be super."

"*Used* to be?"

"Well, last night he cut me off. I mean, that happens, of course, but last night, it seemed . . . I don't know . . . different."

"How?"

"It was as if his mind were somewhere else."

"Has Jack been faithful to you?"

"I think so."

"There's no one you suspect he's been interested in?"

She thought a moment before answering.

"No."

"You hesitated?"

"Oh, I sometimes think he's got a letch on for Marcia Bernstein. And then . . . Well, there's Ben Scovill."

"What about Ben?"

"Jack's very close to him. Too close, I think. I sometimes even wonder if there's some, well, some sort of physical attraction there. I don't mean that Jack's homosexual or anything but . . ."

"An element of bisexuality isn't unusual and certainly not abnormal."

"I suppose that's what I mean. Not that I think anything's going on between them. I genuinely don't, and I don't think there ever will, but . . ." She hesitated. "What's all this got to do with Star Child?"

"You told me that in the second dream, when Raymond more or less 'superseded' Star Child, he appeared—or took on the form of—Jack. Then you said he exposed himself and that his body was repulsive to you. It wouldn't take Jung to suspect that perhaps something has happened to the physical side of your marriage that's disturbed you, and that your subconscious has reacted to it by producing this lurid dream-picture, this transformation of Jack's body into a thing of disgust. You follow me?"

"Yes."

"Do you agree this is a reasonable interpretation?"

She shifted in her chair.

"Well, Jack's been trying some . . . some variations in the past few months."

"Would you mind being more specific?"

"Oral sex . . . and talking about trying the other . . . you know . . ."

"Does this bother you?"

"I guess so. It embarrassed me . . . but Norton, I really think you're off the track, if you don't mind my saying so."

He raised his thick black eyebrows. "How so?"

"You're going about this as a psychiatrist, which is to be expected, trying to explain the dreams in terms of my sexual impulses, or repressions or whatever. Except I don't think they have anything to do with it."

"Dreams are the classic way for the subconscious to release tension."

"But what if they're *not* dreams?"

He leaned forward on the desk.

"Helen, the two dream-beings you've fantasized—Star Child and Raymond—are probably a rather elaborate conceptualization of the good and bad side of something that's bothering you. Now whether it's Jack or not, I'm not sure. But I think we have to proceed on the assumption that your dreams *are* dreams, and not an invasion of your sleeping mind by some exterior force."

"Then do you think what Star Child calls thought projection is an impossibility?"

"I don't say *anything* is an impossibility, and certainly to me, as a psychiatrist, the idea of thought projection is intriguing. You say he told you he generates an electromagnetic field and then transmits his thoughts out on it?"

"Yes, like a super-radio. Does that make any sense?"

"I suppose, Helen, a superior civilization might be able to develop something like that. After all, radio, the telephone and television are all forms of mechanical thought projection, so it's conceivable a technique could be developed to do away with the mechanical intermediaries and transmit thought directly. But I still suggest there's a more plausible explanation to the dreams."

"In other words, you don't think Star Child, whatever he is, exists?"

"No, I honestly don't."

"Do people dream in color?"

"Yes, often. We usually forget the color when we wake up, which is why most of us are under the impression we dream in black and white. But color is natural. There's no reason why our subconscious—our dream-factories—shouldn't use color in the production of our dreams."

"Are people aware of smells in their dreams? I was very conscious of the smell of the apple blossoms in both dreams, and the decomposing flesh . . . well, I'd rather not remember it, but unfortunately I do."

"Awareness of odors in dreams is unusual, but . . ."

"And how is it possible Jack is having these dreams too?" she interrupted. "And you know he must be, even though he's denying it, because otherwise why would he have said what he did to you on the tennis court yesterday? Besides, he was the first one that mentioned Raymond. I didn't know what he was talking about until I had the second dream."

"Well, it's possible his version is true, that he heard you say the name 'Raymond' in your sleep and then perhaps *he* began dreaming about a 'Raymond' through suggestion . . ."

"But that's *not* true," she insisted. "I didn't dream about Raymond that night."

"Dreams are tricky. Sometimes we remember them, more often we don't. Look, Helen, I'm not saying your experience isn't unusual, but I have to approach this from my psychiatric orientation. As I said, Star Child and Raymond apparently represent something your subconscious is trying to express in your dream-content, and apparently Raymond—the 'dark' side of it, if you will—is beginning to repress the Star Child portion. But for me to accept that two entities from outer space are invading your dreams, well, much as the idea intrigues me as a sort of extraterrestrial-life buff . . ." He spread his hands and smiled. ". . . well, let's just say I'm a psychiatrist, not an astro physicist."

"Maybe you're right. I wouldn't be here if I didn't think there might be something wrong with me. But isn't there some way we can test it?"

"Test what?"

"The dreams. To see if they really *are* dreams, or if they're what Star Child says they are."

He thought a moment.

"Perhaps that's not a bad idea," he said, sounding pleased. "And actually there *is* a way we can test it—though it's rather back-handed and I would hardly claim it to be *positive* proof."

"What is it?"

"When we dream, our bodies undergo certain predictable physiological alterations that are testable. If I hooked you up to the electroencephalograph and you went to sleep and had one of these dreams and the EEG did not record as it would a so-called normal dream—well, in that case then we might infer that the dream-experience you had was perhaps something else. Even something as unlikely as a thought projection from an external force . . . Would you be willing to try it?"

"Yes, when?"

"Well, how about tonight? It may take several nights, of course. We don't know when your next Star Child or Raymond dream will occur, but I can assemble the necessary equipment in the lab here, and we can begin as soon as you like. By the way, how is your sleep normally?"

"Excellent."

"You don't use sleeping pills?"

"Never. I don't use anything."

"Good. Sleeping pills profoundly affect normal sleep—for the worse, I might add. Then you'll show up here tonight at, say, ten?"

"Fine."

"How about Jack? What will you tell him?"

She stood up. "The truth," she said. "And if he doesn't like it he can go to hell."

"We know amazingly little about sleep," he said that night as he proceeded to hook up Helen in the lab, "which, considering that it takes up about a third of our lives, is pretty remarkable. It's been only since the Thirties that science has begun to understand what happens to the body and the brain while we're asleep, and we still don't know very much."

She was lying on a bed in a corner of the lab. She was wearing white pajamas, and Norton had already attached most of the electrodes: nine to measure muscular tension (one behind each ear and above each eye, three on her forehead and two on her chin); two on the top of her head for recording brain waves; one on her back for the heartbeat; and one under the arm for body temperature. Now he was placing one next to her nostrils to record breathing.

"How are you feeling?" he asked.

"Like the Bride of Frankenstein," she said glumly.

He smiled.

" 'You were never lovelier.' Anyway, we have found out *some* things about sleep. For instance, we know there are two neurochemicals—serotonin and norepinephrine—which help induce sleep and control our sleep and dream patterns. We know that we fall asleep in stages, the first two stages—light and medium sleep—leading to the third and fourth stages of 'deep' sleep. Each of these stages has characteristic brain waves, heart-beat patterns and so forth. The result is we can always tell where you are by looking at the recorded data. We know that, after you've sunk down to the stage three and four levels, you start to come back up again until you go into the first REM period."

"What's REM?" asked Helen, rather sleepily.

"It stands for 'rapid eye movement.' When we dream, our eyeballs jerk about—whether it's caused by electric impulses from the brain or whether it's because we're actually *watching* our dreams, like an inside-the-skull movie, I don't know. But it happens. And when we pick up those REMs on the machine, we know the subject is probably dreaming. Am I putting you to sleep with all this?"

"A little." She smiled.

"Good. Better a dose of boring information than sleeping pills. All right, you're all hooked up. Now I'll put the jacks in the panel . . ." He proceeded to plug the jacks at the other end of the wires into a panel at the head of the bed. ". . . and you just doze off. I'll be at the other side of the room, monitoring you. If you need anything, just whistle."

"Right." Her eyes were closed.

"And Helen—?"

"Mm?"

"I . . . ." He paused, and his voice seemed almost tender. "I hope this will help."

"Me too."

He looked at her a moment, then wheeled a hospital screen in front of her bed, sectioning her corner off from the rest of the lab. Turning out the lights at that end of the room, he moved to the opposite end and sat down in front of the polygraph and EEG, turning the machines on.

Then he leaned back in the chair and opened a Tab, preparing for a long night's vigil. He seemed curiously tense.

At ten-thirty that same night, a husky young man with a pimply face and long dirty-brown hair, who was hitchhiking west on Route 44, saw a car slow down and stop. He broke into a run, and, when he reached the green Dodge, the driver, who was about his age, said, "Where are you going? I couldn't read your sign."

"Albany."

"I can take you near the state border."

"Great."

Taking off his backpack, he tossed it in the rear along with the piece of cardboard on which he'd lettered ALBANY. Then he climbed in front. Ben Scovill shifted to Drive and got back on the highway, which had little traffic.

"Thanks a lot. I appreciate the lift."

"No problem. Where you from?"

"Katonah."

"In New York?"

"Yeah."

"What are you doing in Connecticut?"

"I was seeing this girl I know in Avon."

"Near Hartford?"

"That's right. I started for Albany this afternoon, but I've had shitty luck with rides. I was about to call it a night and sack out in a field."

Ben glanced sideways at his passenger. Beat-up jeans with matching shirt. A year out of style, at least.

"What's in Albany?"

"The State University. I'm getting there a couple of weeks early to try and line up a job. This is my second year."

"Like it?"

"It's all right. You in college?"

"No. I mean, I was supposed to start somewhere this year, but I decided to screw it. Who needs college?"

"You've got a point. Mind if I smoke? I mean, a cigarette?"

"Go ahead."

He pulled a pack of Camels from his shirt pocket and held it out.

"Want one?"

"No thanks," said Ben. "I don't smoke. I get my kicks better ways."

"Like?"

Ben smiled slightly.

"You know. Things."

The passenger looked at him sharply as he pushed in the lighter. After he'd lit the cigarette, he leaned back and exhaled. "My name's Roger, which is a dumb-ass name. What's yours?"

"Ben. Not much better."

Roger grinned.

"Oh, I don't know. Ben Franklin—it's better than Roger."

"Maybe."

They drove a quarter-mile in silence.

"Nice car," said Roger.

"Thanks. My old man died a couple of months ago, so I, you know, inherited it."

"Yeah? I'm sorry to hear it. I mean, about your old man." He flipped the cigarette out the window and added, "Wish to God *my* old man would die."

"Is he a pain in the ass?"

"He's a fucking drunk."

"No kidding?"

"He puts bourbon on his goddam corn flakes." He shook his head. "So, who's left? Your mother?"

"No one," said Ben. "I live alone."

"Yeah? I'd like that."

"It's all right."

"No hassle, no one to tell you to pick up your damn socks . . ."

Silence for a while as Roger watched his benefactor, whose face was illuminated by the green dashlights. Then he said, "So what are these things you get your kicks from? You got someone you shack up with?"

Ben shrugged.

"Well, they come and go."

Roger laughed.

"Sounds like you got it all wrapped up. You, uh, smoke? I mean, like, *not* cigarettes?"

Ben didn't answer for a moment. Then:

"Sure. Sometimes. You have to be careful in Connecticut."

"It's a lot better here than in New York. In New York the cops bug your asshole."

"I know, but still."

"That's why I went to Avon. You know what I mean?"

Ben looked at him.

"You mean in the backpack?"

"That's right. Like some? I mean, as a gift. You know, because you're giving me a ride and all that shit."

"I wouldn't say no."

Roger started to lean over the seat to get the backpack.

"Wait a minute," said Ben. "Tell you what. Why don't you sack out at my place tonight and you can, you know, smoke a few joints. Then in the morning I can bring you back to 44 and you'll have a fresh start."

"Hey, man, you've got a deal," said Roger, settling back in his seat with a satisfied smile. "That'll be all right. In fact"—and he laughed—"I was hoping you'd ask. I could sure use a bed."

"I've got a nice cot in the cellar," said Ben.

Roger looked at him rather curiously, then pulled out the pack of Camels to light another cigarette.

2

The low, diapason pedal-tones of the opening theme of the Bach *Passacaglia* rumbled from beneath the choir, where the organ's bass pipes were concealed, as Helen walked slowly down the center aisle of the school chapel. The handsome Georgian-style building was dark except for the light at the organ console in the choir behind the altar, which threw its white glow up on the thin face of Sarah Blake. Her hands helped support her on the bench as her feet played the majestic theme on the pedal board: she seemed absorbed by the music, unaware of Helen's presence. Then, as the opening theme concluded, she put her hands on the middle keyboard, and the thin answering theme issued from the flute ranks concealed behind the false organ pipes above the choir. The beauty and purity of the music was magically relaxing. Helen, enchanted by it, eased herself into a pew and listened.

After a few minutes, as the variations of the *Passacaglia* theme intertwined, weaving a gorgeous pattern of sound, she heard soft footsteps on the slate aisle. Turning around, she saw a man coming toward her from the rear of the chapel. As he came closer in the dimness, she saw it was Jack.

He was smiling at her.

She smiled back and scooted over on the wooden

pew to make room for him. He sat beside her and took her hand.

"What are you doing here?" he whispered. "I thought you were with Norton."

"I was," she answered, frowning slightly. "I mean, I am. This is a dream."

"No it isn't."

She looked more confused.

"It isn't?"

"Of course not. You're getting hung up on dreams."

Then he turned his face back to the altar. The faint light from the organ edged his profile as she looked at him. She had thought it was a dream, but now she wasn't sure. She tried to remember how she got in the chapel, but she couldn't. The uncomfortable thought occurred to her that she was no longer capable of differentiating her dream-life from reality.

Except her dream-life so far had been bizarre, if not grotesque, and this was so peaceful in contrast. As Jack put his arm affectionately around her shoulder, she relaxed in the warmth of his body, aware that this was the first time in almost two days that she hadn't felt hostility from—and toward—her husband. This made her happy. If it was a dream, it was a nice one, for once. If it was reality, it was delightful.

She put her head on his chest and closed her eyes, her ears flooded with Bach, her heart with peace.

"Jack," she whispered. "I love you."

He leaned down and kissed her forehead, his right hand squeezing her arm lovingly.

"I love you," he replied.

"I'm sorry we fought."

"It was my fault. I *have* been boozing too much. I'll cut down from now on."

She looked up.

"Will you? Really?"

"Really. Scout's Honor."

Smiling, she kissed his mouth. His breath was sweet

and fresh, his kiss warm. Her old love for him seemed as sweet and fresh as his breath. She wanted him with a desire so suddenly intense, it surprised her.

"Let's go home," she whispered.

"I want to hear the music. It's beautiful."

"I know. But I want to . . . you know."

He kissed her again.

"Let's do it here."

"In the chapel?"

"Why not?" He started unbuttoning her blouse.

"Nobody's going to come in here. And, if Sarah sees us, it'll give her a kick. Come on."

"Jack . . ."

She had no resistance. She wanted him. Besides, the idea of making love in the church strangely appealed to her. And yet it was perverse, a sexual blasphemy. She was surprised at her thoughts; something told her to beware. Gently, she pushed him away.

"Darling, we can't. Be serious."

"Making love is part of the psychic force of the universe," he whispered. "There's nothing 'wrong' with it, you know that. Making love in God's house is like the ultimate prayer."

She giggled. "You nut. Since when have you ever believed in prayer—*or* God?"

"Now."

He leaned over her, kissing her, and gently forced her back down on the pew. She tried to resist him, but found she either couldn't, or didn't want to. The *Passacaglia* had finished, and the magnificent double fugue had begun. The music seemed erotic, for no reason at all. Reason, in fact, had vanished.

Now she didn't care where she was, she almost didn't care who did it.

She started tearing at his clothes.

He was laughing.

"You're really turned on, aren't you?" he whispered.

She said nothing. She was sitting up now, her legs

on the floor again, pulling his sportshirt off him. The sight of his flesh, dim in the organ light, made her forget where she was. She put her mouth on his right nipple and sucked as her right hand pushed inside his pants to squeeze his genitals. She felt his penis stiffen against her fingers, she wanted to impale herself on it.

She felt something crawl on her foot.

She looked down in the darkness beneath the pew and saw the two eyes of a huge rat looking at her. She scrambled up onto the seat of the pew, disentangling herself from Jack, who was watching her.

She heard the scurrying, the nails against the slate floor of the chapel rustling in eerie counterpoint to the organ music. Then they were on the back of the pew in front of her: three of them running down the rounded wooden spine. One of them stopped in front of her and stared. She froze, staring back at the two eyes.

"Jack," she whispered, "get me out of here . . ."

She turned to look at him. He was gone.

The chapel, she realized, was alive with rats. Thousands of them. She not only heard them, now she could see them, swarming in the darkness down the aisles, running under the pews, climbing up on the altar.

The organ music suddenly stopped, the organ light blinked out, and she was alone in the black chapel.

Alone with the rats.

She began to scream. She stood up on the seat, she felt them run over her feet. She tried to kick them off, but there were too many. One pounced on her shoulder. She yelled and hit it with her hand. It squealed as it hit the pew behind her with a thud.

A huge blue flame flared up on the altar. It was almost ten feet high and flooded the chapel with its cold light. In the middle of it slowly appeared the outlines of a skull, the dark holes of the hollow eye sockets black against the blue of the flame.

"I am Raymond," the Voice said, slowly, with the ominous deepness of an organ tone. "The one and only god, the son of Starfire, the Creator." A bedlam of squeaks from the rats.

"Worship me or be destroyed."

"I don't believe you!" she cried. "You're a fake, I don't believe you!"

The rats were chewing at her ankles now, and the pain chewed at her brain. As she screamed the organ broke into a manic pealing, a thunderous cacophony of maddening discords. She held her hands to her ears and shut her eyes, trying to disconnect herself from the scene by stopping the input to her brain.

She felt two hands on her shoulders, shaking her.

"Helen! Helen!"

Norton Akroyd was leaning over her, shaking her.

She opened her eyes, looked into his intense face, and continued to scream. He slapped her. The sting and pain jolted her into silence. She threw her arms around him and sobbed.

"Oh God, oh God . . ."

"What *was* it?"

"Oh Norton, please *please* . . . for God's sake, don't let that happen to me again. *Please*. Don't let it happen again . . ."

"Was it Raymond?"

"Yes . . . oh Christ, yes . . . What does he want? Why is he doing this to me? *Why?*"

As he held her, the EEG wires springing from her head like frightened hairs, Norton Akroyd wasn't sure how to answer her. After a while, she put her head back on the pillow, trying to compose herself. Her eyes closed with exhaustion, she said, "He's trying to kill me through the dreams."

Norton sat on the edge of the bed a moment before replying. Then, simply: "They're not dreams."

Her eyes opened.

"What do you mean?"

"You've been asleep only ten minutes," he said. "You were nowhere near the stage of sleep when you would begin dreaming. I don't know what it was you had, but it certainly wasn't a dream."

She said nothing. She merely stared at him with her bloodshot eyes.

For the first time in her life, she wished she were dead.

"It belonged to my great-great-grandmother, who was supposed to be a sorceress," said Ben Scovill as he handed the curiously shaped branding iron to Jack Bradford. They were both in the attic of Ben's house standing over the rusty trunk where the Japanese sword had been stored since that day, early in 1946, when Ben's father had returned from overseas.

"What is it?" asked Jack, taking the black instrument, which was about three feet long and crudely hammered out of iron.

"It's supposed to be the Star of Satan. See at the end? It's got five points—a pentagram. The idea was— or at least this is the story my mother told me—that the members of the coven would hold a black mass to try and raise the Devil. And part of the ceremony was to offer a sacrifice to Satan. Well, they were too chicken to kill anyone, so they'd use this thing instead."

"You mean they branded *people?*" said Jack distastefully.

"That's right. On the ass. Branding was pretty common in the old days around here. They'd brand them on the ass, and that would make the woman—or man—a 'child of the Evil One.' It also gave the others a sadistic kick, and Raymond has told me that a lot of the so-called dark religions were tied up with sado-masochism. You game to try it?"

"What do you mean?"

"You know damn well what I mean."

Jack looked at the branding iron in his hands.

"What are you afraid of?"

"Myself . . . the police . . . you . . . I guess . . ."

Ben laughed.

"Oh come on. We're friends, after all. As for the police, they haven't bothered me."

"That's because no one knows the two women are dead. Not yet. They think they're missing——"

"What kind of a god do you think Raymond is?" interrupted Ben. "Do you think he's like Jesus? Jesus couldn't protect his disciples . . . he couldn't even protect *himself*. But Raymond will have power: *real* power. When he comes, he's bringing something that will give him all the power in the world—all the money in the world. I know what it is, he told me. It's the power of the sun! Think of it: the power of the sun and other stars, the ultimate power of the universe! And you think he's going to let some cop hurt his followers? The people who love and worship him? Jack, use your head. We're safe, nothing can hurt us. We're beyond ordinary things."

Jack looked dubious. "What do you mean, 'the power of the sun'?"

"Just that. Raymond said he's bringing the secret of something called thermonuclear fusion."

"Then who's Star Child that Helen is dreaming about? She says he's some kid who claims *he's* bringing the secret of thermonuclear fusion. It's not much of a secret. Half the damn universe seems to be rushing to bring it to us."

"Star Child is the other one," said Ben. "Raymond told me about him. He's a false god, and Raymond will destroy him."

"How do we know he's false?"

"Because the Master *told* me. Come on. Let's go downstairs."

Again, Jack Bradford looked at the cruel instrument in his hands. His heart was pounding, but he told himself it was fear. Could it have been anticipation too?

"You know," said Ben softly, "Raymond not only

protects the ones who follow him, he also punishes those who don't."

Jack looked up. "Is that a threat?"

Ben slowly nodded "yes." Jack hesitated, then he started toward the attic door.

"We can use the coal from the furnace to heat up the iron," Ben said as they started down the stairs.

"All right, let's assume Raymond exists. Let's assume he's an intelligent . . . 'force,' I suppose, is the best word . . . that is invading your sleeping mind by a method of highly sophisticated thought transmission. By the way, I think it's significant that he seems to be able to enter only your *sleeping* mind."

"Why?" said Helen, who was sitting on the edge of the bed in the laboratory sipping a cup of tea Norton Akroyd had made her. The electrodes had been removed from her head and body.

"Because presumably your waking mind would put up too much resistance to the thought projection," said Norton, stirring his tea as he leaned against the lab wall, watching her closely, measuring his words as he spoke. "It's like hypnosis. The hypnotist has to lull the conscious mind into at least an early stage of sleep before he can exert his will on the subject. The same applies to Raymond. Apparently he has to wait until you're asleep before he can enter your mind. The enormous difference is that, once he's in, he seems to be able to do extraordinary things."

"But what's the *point* of the extraordinary things?" she said, wearily. "To scare me to death? Star Child said Jack might kill me, but I suspect Raymond's going to do the job himself."

"No, I think it's something else. We have to take what he says in the dreams at face value. 'Worship me or be destroyed'—isn't that it?"

"Yes."

"Then perhaps he's using a technique of psychosexual terror to frighten you into this worship of him. Not meaning to sound blasphemous, but it's not entirely dissimilar to the technique God used in the Old Testament: the God of vengeance, the God of terror, the God of plagues and torments. This Raymond force may not be a god, but he apparently wants to be worshiped like one and he's using a time-tried method to accomplish it."

"But why the use of sex? Or, rather, why is he trying to make sex repulsive to me? First the horrible *thing* in the graveyard; then in the chapel, just when I was wanting Jack so desperately, the rats . . ."

She shuddered.

"Again, I can only guess," said Norton. "But sex is one of the most powerful forces in our minds, and perhaps Raymond is tapping that power-source to manipulate your will. The fact that he takes the form of your husband may suggest that he's trying to divert your love for Jack to him. Also your fear of Jack. Love, fear or hate. The classic opposites. Control them and we control the essence of a person's emotions."

"But he's in *Jack's* mind too! What does that mean?"

"Perhaps he uses different methods to make Jack fear and worship him."

She thought a while, then said:

"What time is it?"

He checked his watch.

"Twenty minutes before midnight."

"I'm going home."

"But you were going to spend the night here . . ."

"I've learned everything I can here. I've learned that they aren't dreams. Now I've got to talk to Jack. He *has* to tell me what's been happening in his dreams. We have to be honest with each other before . . . well——"

"But do you think it's safe to go? If you're right and there *is* the possibility . . ."

"I have to face him sometime, don't I? It might as

well be now." She started to return to the bathroom, where she had left her clothes. "Besides," she said at the door, "there's a gun in the house. Jack bought it last year in case there were prowlers. We're so isolated up there. I'll try to make sure *I* have the gun before I start asking questions."

She went into the bathroom to change.

A half hour later she pulled up her tiny gray Toyota in front of her now-darkened house and got out. He wouldn't be expecting her, which was good. She closed the car door as quietly as she could and went to the front entrance, pulling her housekey from her change purse. It was a balmy night, with a melon slice of a new moon rising over the top of Rock Mountain where she could see, even in the darkness, that more trees had been cut down. She inserted the key in the lock and opened the door. The living room was dark, quiet. She closed the door and turned on a lamp. She went into the dining room and opened the corner cupboard. She reached her hand behind the stack of Quimper plates and felt the hard steel of the Smith & Wesson. For a second, she reconsidered. My God, he was her husband! Could she seriously believe he might be a physical threat to her?

But he *isn't* my husband, she told herself. His mind has apparently been turned inside out by some alien force . . . something. She took hold of the gun, pulled it out of the cupboard and put it in her pocketbook.

She returned to the living room, went to the stairs and called, "Jack?"

Silence.

"Jack, I'm home."

She hurried up the stairs and looked in both bedrooms. Empty.

It was past midnight, and her husband was gone.

She went downstairs again and sat on the sofa, watching the front door. She had no idea where he had gone, but she was determined to wait up for him.

With the gun.

3

Jack Bradford had gotten half-drunk, but he knew he would remember this bizarre evening the rest of his life. It was a scene from the Spanish Inquisition, this cellar room with the terrified young hitchhiker tied by his wrists to the ceiling beam, his mouth gagged, his feet strapped together by a leather belt, his eyes showing incredulous fear as he watched Ben heat the branding iron in the steel bucket filled with red-hot coals. The Spanish Inquisition, and he, Jack Bradford, the peaceful English master, was Torquemada. No, wrong: he wasn't the Grand Inquisitor, he was the Chief Torturer, ready to break the victim's body by administering the bone-smashing strappado or the agonizing aselli. And, like the Inquisition, it was all being done in the name of religion, except what a difference in theology! The torture was not even putatively for the benefit of the heretic's soul, but rather for the gratification of the torturer. And then, afterward, what? The victim would be "delivered over to the secular arm," in the genteel phraseology of the Inquisition, for a love-death, in the Wagnerian phraseology of Raymond. A love-death. Could he possibly do it? Was it even *remotely* possible he could?

As he raised the bottle of red wine to his lips, watching the boy, he confessed to himself the answer was at least a qualified "yes."

There could be no question of Ben having misgivings. He had enjoyed half-braining the hitchhiker with the fireplace poker, he had enjoyed tying him to the beam, he was enjoying the heating of the branding iron. Periodically, he would look at Roger, whose blue-jean shirt was soaked with hoops of sweat, and smile. Ben was indeed enjoying himself.

"I think it's hot enough," he said, lifting the iron from the coals. The five-pointed star on the end, about three inches at its greatest width, was smoking and glowing a dull red. "Are you ready?"

Jack took another swig of the red wine, then set the half-gallon bottle on the dirt floor, wiping his mouth with his shirt sleeve. He was weaving slightly.

"Where . . . ?" he asked.

Ben put the branding iron back on the coals and removed the plaid oven-gloves from his hands.

He placed his finger on his forehead. Roger, seeing this, began jerking with fear. Jack winced.

"I can't do *that*."

"Can't you?" said Ben, tossing him the gloves. Jack caught them and held them, uncertainly, then looked at the hitchhiker. It took little imagination to guess what he was thinking.

Ben sat down on the edge of the cot, which he had moved from the center of the cellar to a side wall. Now he said to Jack, "Raymond says Christianity has been dying for centuries, and it was always a false religion. It said man could be redeemed. It held out hope, while at the same time causing millions of deaths in religious wars and persecutions. Our new religion at least doesn't hold out false hopes. It says we are what we are and that we should be proud of it."

"Raymond has done this. It's not what I am . . ." he slurred with boozy anger.

Ben laughed. "Raymond has liberated you, that's all. Well?"

Jack didn't move for a moment. He looked first at Ben, then Roger, whose face was streaming with sweat.

Jack put on the oven-gloves and walked to the coal bucket. He took the end of the branding iron with both hands and lifted it. He looked for a moment at the steaming star, a look of fear mixed with disbelieving excitement.

He turned and, holding the smoking star in front of him, started toward Roger.

Love-death. Pain. The pleasures of de Sade. Murder. Violence. The ideas swirled in his mind, mingling with the fumes of the wine, dulling logic, releasing the sewer gas in his soul. By the time he was standing in front of Roger, holding the brand in front of his forehead, the hitchhiker was no longer a human being but a thing, something to give him pleasure. Even a sacrifice to a new god.

Suddenly, the few restraints left in his mind vanished. He *wanted* to do it. He touched the red-hot star on Roger, just above the left eye. The head jerked back as the knees knifed up, narrowly missing Jack's groin. A stench and a muted sound of pain came from the throat.

Then the body slumped into unconsciousness, head dangling to one side.

Jack stared, marveled. There were no more doubts in his mind. The "yes" was no longer qualified. As Ben had said, it was a release, a freedom. Ben came up beside him, and took his arm. "Welcome to the brotherhood," he whispered. "And to Raymond's love."

Then he leaned forward and put his mouth on Jack's.

PART III

The Visions

1

It was a Mary Petty scene.

The well-tended tennis court with the four people in white playing doubles. The green lawns of the campus (here and there patched with brown from the late-summer lack of rain) spotted with stately trees. The empty red-brick buildings of the school interspersed with neat, white faculty houses. The river flowing lazily at its lowest level of the year. The bees swarming around the newly flowering stock. The sunny blue sky.

Helen Bradford sat on the grass beneath the maple tree watching her husband and Ben Scovill play Jeremy and Marcia Bernstein. Jack was at the net, Ben was back, and they were ahead two sets. Ben, the natural athlete, was good. Too good, in fact.

Helen had come to hate him.

She saw Norton Akroyd walking across the lawn toward her. He was wearing neat khaki pants and a red-striped sportshirt that made him look unusually young. He sat next to her in the shade and said, "I haven't seen you for three days. What happened?"

"Nothing," she said.

"Did you and he talk it out?"

"No. When I got home, he wasn't there. He didn't come back till the next morning."

"Where was he?"

She watched Ben serve.

"He *said* he went to Hartford . . . that he was restless and wanted a drive. I told him he was lying, and he just shrugged."

"Why do you think he lied?"

She hesitated.

"I'm not sure. He won't talk about the dreams, either. He's still pretending he never had them."

"Have you had any more?"

"No. Nothing. Neither Star Child nor Raymond. Maybe they're on strike."

The psychiatrist smiled.

"Do you still feel you're in danger?"

"Yes."

"Maybe you should go away for a while."

"Going away won't solve anything." She waved a fly from her nose. "Besides, there's something new in my life." This, very dryly.

"What?"

"Ben Scovill. He and Jack have suddenly gotten even chummier. I think that's where he was that night. At Ben's house."

Norton Akroyd looked at Ben, who was running after a corner shot.

"Do you think they . . . ?" He didn't finish the sentence, though his meaning was clear.

"I don't know for certain, but *something's* going on in that house."

Silence for a while as they watched the game. Then Norton said, "I did a little investigating of my own. I have a friend who works at the National Radio Observatory in Green Bank, West Virginia. I called him and asked if he would search the sky in the direction of Tau Ceti and see if he picked up anything unusual. I think he thought I was a bit nuts for asking but he said he would."

"It was a good idea."

"Well, I thought it was worth trying."

"And?"

"He called me back last night. He said there was nothing."

She thought about this. "Then Star Child must be lying. I wonder why."

"I don't know."

The game finished and the four players left the court to sit in the shade for a rest. As Ben came up, he smiled at Helen. "Why don't you get your racquet, Mrs. Bradford? You could play the next set with Jack."

"No thanks. And since you seem to be on a first-name basis with my husband, why don't you call me Helen?"

He wiped his face and continued to smile despite the obvious hostility of her tone.

"Okay, Helen."

As she watched him, she wondered for the hundredth time what had gone on in Ben's house that night—for she was certain that's where Jack had gone. She didn't *want* to believe they had become lovers: the thought made her miserable, and also furious. Still, she had to admit they were acting the role. Suddenly, Ben seemed everywhere. Jack had asked him to dinner two nights before (and during the meal they had talked mostly to each other, practically ignoring her); Ben had "dropped by" the house the next day for lunch; Jack had "gone to town" the day before for four hours, except that she had seen his car turn up the mountain road toward Ben's house rather than turn south toward town. And then, this morning, tennis anyone? There was Ben with his tennis racquet, smiling, all gleaming white and gorgeous. Ben, Ben, Ben. She had never given any thought to Ben's sexuality— she had always assumed he was normal—and yet that slyness about him . . . could it be that the slyness was a cover, a façade to hide the truth? And if Raymond had turned Jack's mind inside out, which was the way she thought of it, why couldn't he have turned Ben's as well?

The house. Ben's house. Her intuition told her something was there, something Ben and Jack knew and she didn't. She wanted to go into that house but she was afraid . . . of what, she wasn't sure.

The group had been chatting amiably, and now Jeremy Bernstein suggested another set. When they returned to the court, Helen got to her feet.

"Where are you going?" asked Norton.

"To Ben's house."

"Why?" he asked, surprised. "What's there?"

"I don't know, but I'm going to take a look. Tell Jack I've gone home—if he's interested enough to ask."

He watched her as she walked across the lawn to her Toyota.

She went home first, got out of the car and looked inside her big leather shoulderbag to make sure the gun was there. Not that she believed she would actually need to use it, but its presence was reassuring. Then she began walking up the hill behind the house— she didn't want to risk having her car seen entering Ben's drive. As she climbed the slope, her mind tried to grapple with the question that had been plaguing her for days: what to do with her husband? Perhaps Norton was right. Perhaps she should just leave. Certainly her situation was becoming increasingly untenable. A husband whose personality had apparently been changed into something new, a husband she suspected might try to cause her physical harm . . . could she continue to live this way? And yet could she just walk away from her home and the husband she still felt she loved? Except he wasn't her husband Jack any more. He was more Raymond. Raymond. And Star Child? If Star Child had lied, if he weren't from Tau Ceti, then where was he from and what *was he?* Had everything he told her in the dreams—the dreams that weren't dreams—been lies? And if so, why?

She reached the top and stopped for breath. She looked around. Ben had certainly done a job on the trees. He must have cut down at least ten, sawing them into firelogs and piling them neatly at the side of the clearing. A clearing almost, she judged, thirty feet square. It was curious that he would go to the top of the mountain to cut trees when there were so many of them down the north face, closer to his house. She remembered how Jack had snapped at her when she saw the first tree being cut, and the strange feeling then that there was something conspiratorial about the tree-cutting. . . . Ridiculous . . . but true. Conspiracies. Since she had started having dreams she could still think of this in no other way. Everything had become a conspiracy. She felt she was in a hall of mirrors where everything was distorted, reflected crazily, hidden. She knew that the beginning of paranoia was the idea that the rest of the world was conspiring against you, and yet she couldn't help but feel it. But what *was* the conspiracy? Whatever reason could Ben have to cut down the trees except to make firewood?

She started down the north face of the mountain toward Ben's house. The top of Rock Mountain . . . was it coincidence that the three people living closest to the top of the mountain apparently had been contacted (afflicted) by either Star Child or Raymond?

She wondered if Star Child and Raymond were the same entity, or two faces of the same personality. *What* personality? And if Star Child was supposed to bring the gift of thermonuclear fusion to earth, why invade her dreams in the guise of Raymond?

It was also possible she was mad. She tried to confront it. She had told herself she wasn't when Norton had confirmed that the apparent dreams were something other than conventional, known dreams. But maybe she was anyway. And maybe Norton was crazy in his interpretation. Maybe, despite his heated denial, he *was* trying some sort of hypnotic thought projection on her and Jack and Ben to prove his theory and—what? Win the Nobel Prize? Or perhaps merely satisfy his ego? But that was so improbable. Besides, how could he *do* it? Norton was no mad scientist; he was merely a psychiatrist with a theory about human nature, a theory that seemed to be in the process of being proven by her husband in spectacular fashion.

Jack. The real Jack she had loved, that she still loved. If Jack had become someone else, someone alien to her and himself, she had to try to help him, or save him, or something . . . But how? She didn't know how to help herself anymore. Except the gun.

She was next to the red barn now, close to the house, and even in the warm sunlight the place seemed rather menacing. Or was she imagining it? She walked across the yard to the front porch and looked through a window. The house seemed deserted. Naturally. What did she expect? Raymond?

She went to the front door and tried it. Locked. Did she dare try to force her way in? She told herself she didn't dare not to. But the door looked strong. She thought a moment, then went around the house to the back door. This, too, was locked, but a window next to it was open, letting in the breeze (unlike the front of the house, the rear windows were plastic-free). She shoved it all the way up and managed to pull herself over the sill.

The kitchen was a mess, and momentarily she wondered if the house also had rats, like the chapel in her dreams . . . her fantasy . . . Shuddering slightly at the memory, she walked into the living room. She had never been in the house before so she didn't know where to look or, for that matter, what to look for. Silence, except for the ticking of a wooden clock on the mantel. She looked in the back room. Nothing. She went upstairs and into his bedroom. Bette Midler shouted silently at her as the Guru Maharaj Ji contemplated her, smugly benign, and Peter Fonda sat mute on his motorcycle. The unmade bed, the papers and magazines strewn everywhere. What did she expect to find? She had no idea. She was even beginning to feel rather ashamed. After all, she was breaking and entering.

She looked in the other bedrooms, which yielded nothing except dust, then returned to the kitchen. It was then she saw the trapdoor in the corner. She went to it and pulled it open. Finding the light switch, she started down the wooden stairs.

Then she knew she had found it.

A makeshift altar. She went across the dirt floor to the shawled chest and looked at the candles and the incense bowl. A *chapel.* He had turned his cellar into a kind of chapel . . . to Raymond? It was bizarre. Was *this* what Jack had been doing here? He and Ben, actually praying to an unseen God, kneeling on the dirt floor in front of this absurd altar praying to their absurd god, perhaps . . . she looked around the room and stared at the cot against the wall . . . perhaps doing something else . . .

She felt a rush of anger and jealousy. Ben! That miserable little bastard, actually stealing her husband . . . that sick, perverted . . . And then she told herself that was stupid. Not Ben and not Jack. It was Raymond . . .

She saw the blanket chest and went over to it. Opening it, she looked inside. A huge, white owl head stared up at her. She lifted the thing out and examined it.

Setting it on the floor, she saw the harem pants and held them up. *Harem* pants? She took them to the center of the room and held them under the light. The white cotton had been splattered with something which had been scrubbed out, and yet the stain remained, a dark reddish shadow.

She heard the front door open upstairs. She froze. Footsteps squeaked the floorboards over her head as the door was closed. She watched the ceiling, following the sound of the footsteps as they crossed the living room and went into the kitchen. Whoever it was would see the open trapdoor . . . she cursed herself for not closing it as she looked around the cellar trying to find someplace to hide. Behind the furnace? It was too late now. Whoever it was was at the trapdoor. She wanted to scream away her fear. She told herself it was Raymond, Raymond who knew every move she made . . . she envisioned a hideous thing standing at the top of the stairs—a slimy, repulsive, monstrous thing . . .

She saw the tennis shoes on the top step as Ben started down the stairs. He didn't look at all surprised to see her.

"Hello, Helen. Having fun?"

She watched him as he came down the stairs. When he reached the bottom, he noticed the opened blanket chest.

"I see you've found my prop department. How do you like those pants? I made them myself."

"Why?" she said carefully. She sensed Ben wasn't there to make small talk.

"Oh, for a little home theatrical I staged here the other night."

"What are the stains?" she asked quietly.

"Blood." He said it casually. "The blood of a woman named Betty Fredericks, from Fairfax. She's buried about a foot behind you."

She looked behind her at the dirt floor. It seemed no different from the rest of the floor. She turned back to him.

"You're lying."

"Remember Judy Siebert, the girl who's been missing for a week? She's in front of the altar. This cellar's turning into a regular graveyard—I don't even charge for the plots." He didn't smile when he said it.

"Why would you kill them—*if* you did?"

"They were sacrifices. To the Master, Raymond."

She put the pants on the bed.

"Then he's *not* a dream," she said softly.

"He's very real. He'll be arriving soon, on top of the mountain. That's why I cut down the trees. And when he arrives, it's going to be a whole new ball game."

"What are you talking about?"

"Raymond will change the world." He said it with conviction. "The way he's changed me. And your devoted husband. We're both apostles now, you know."

"No, I didn't know."

He leaned against the stair rail, crossing his arms over his chest, watching her with a pleasant expression.

"We're going to be very important in this new religion. And it's not going to be like the last time—you know, 'turn the other cheek.' "

"So what is this wonderful new religion about?"

"Sex, self-gratification, love, death. It's already happening. I mean, all over the world people are killing because people *like* to kill. It's the greatest pleasure. All the Master asks is that we do it in his name."

"If you really believe that crap, you're disgusting."

"And your husband? Do you think he's disgusting too?"

She didn't answer.

"Three nights ago," he went on, "I picked up a hitchhiker named Roger—I never got to find out his last name. I brought him back here. We tied him to that ceiling beam over your head . . ." He pointed.

" 'We'?"

"Your *husband,* Jack, and I. Then Jack branded him on the forehead, then he screwed him. . . ."

"Stop it!"

"Then he cut his throat."

"You're crazy . . . I don't believe a word you say—"

"Oh? Then you don't believe that Jack and I are lovers?"

"You filthy . . ."

"Sticks and stones!"

His mocking cut her short. Regaining some of her composure, she started toward the stairs.

"Where are you going?" He was moving in front of her.

"To the police."

"Now, you don't really think I'm going to let you do that."

"You don't have any choice." She pulled the gun from her pocket and pointed it at him. He looked at it, rather surprised.

"What about Jack?" he said. "Do you want your husband to go to jail?"

"Neither of you will probably go to jail, but you're going to spend a long time with a good psychiatrist."

"You stupid cunt, do you really think psychiatrists can equal the power of Raymond? Do you think the police can? He's a god! He *is* God! He's all-powerful, he's coming to our world and nothing can stop him."

And then he was moving toward her, trying to grab hold of the gun. She fired point-blank at his chest, but he kept on coming, propelled by the momentum of his charge. She fired again, then again. He stopped, a confused look on his face, then half-turned and pitched forward onto the dirt floor, his head landing an inch from her toes.

For a moment she just stared at him, mumbling, "Oh God, oh God . . ." She knelt beside him. Putting the gun on the floor, she reached out to touch him, almost fearfully. She turned him over on his back. He was still alive. His blue eyes looked up at her as his lips tried to form words.

Finally they stopped moving.

She stood up. She was shaking. She backed away from the body, started for the stairs. She stopped and went back to pick up the gun. Then she ran to the stairs and started for the kitchen.

Halfway up, she stopped again to take one more look at him.

Then she went to the kitchen, slammed the trapdoor shut and let herself out the back door.

The "dream" had now become reality. She too had killed, and now she was part of the nightmare. As she ran down the drive to Rock Mountain Road, she told herself she had to do it, that he would have killed her if she hadn't fired the gun.

It didn't matter. She had killed him. Would anyone believe her version?

She was afraid to go home and face Jack but she needed to get her car. And then where would she go? The police? Yes, of course she'd have to tell the police, and they would go to the cellar and dig up the graves and arrest Jack, and then the papers and television would have a field-day . . . Mass Murders in New England, Jealous Wife Shoots Husband's Male Lover . . . That is, if they believed her. But how could they? Raymond was unbelievable.

She was crying now, half-running, half-stumbling up Rock Mountain Road, the gun still in her hand. She would have to tell the police, *have* to, but not just yet. She needed time to think, to talk to someone, but not Jack . . . no, not Jack . . . God knows what he would do when he found out she had killed his precious Ben. . . . It was true. Jack and Ben had been lovers, Jack and Ben had apparently murdered an innocent boy in the name of Raymond, the god they believed was coming to earth to change the world.

Finally she reached her Toyota, exhausted. She got in the car, started the engine, drove back to Rock Mountain Road, then headed down the hill to the campus to see Norton Akroyd.

She found him in his apartment, where he had returned from the tennis court to work on his book. On his desk was a photograph of a New York mugging victim who had been gratuitously shot in the head by the mugger who'd taken his wallet containing twelve dollars. She closed the door of the apartment, went to a sofa and collapsed.

"What did you find?" he asked.

"The answer to what happened to Judy Siebert."

He sat down at his desk, bewilderment on his face.

"Norton," she said, "if you're mad enough—or skilled enough—to cause these dreams, then you've proved your point. Because three people who have had them—myself and Jack and Ben Scovill, and all of us have committed murders."

He said nothing. She sat up, brushing her hair back from her forehead, and went on: "Ben came down into his cellar while I was there. He told me there were three bodies buried there: people he and Jack had murdered. When I tried to go to the police, he attacked me and I shot him."

"But I'm not responsible," he said. "It's crazy to think I could induce these dreams . . . I've *told* you that . . ."

"Then the only alternative is: Raymond is real. Ben thought he was. He said he and Jack were apostles in some crazy new religion that worships Raymond, who's arriving on top of Rock Mountain to celebrate the beginning of a new era in history. Now, figure *that* out."

"I . . . I can't."

"Neither can I."

"Are you going to tell the police?"

"I know I should."

"What does that mean?"

"That I'm afraid they won't believe me. God knows why they should. If I go to them now and tell them I've killed someone because something from outer space or a new god or whatever the hell he is has taken over my husband's mind, they'll lock me up and throw away the key. Besides, I can't do it to Jack if he's not really responsible for what he's done."

"But Helen, that's what I was saying that night at your party: our characters *can* be altered."

"Oh God, I'm not talking about theories now. I'm talking about *people*. It would ruin Jack's life."

"What if he kills someone else?"

She sighed as she leaned her elbow on the sofa arm and wearily rubbed her forehead. "I know; it's a terrible risk. But I still can't go to the police—at least, not right now. I have to try and think this out."

"What about Ben's body?"

"Jack will find it. Let *him* go to the police. I doubt that he will."

Norton thought a moment. "Perhaps you're right," he finally said. "Perhaps it's better not to do anything for the moment. But you probably shouldn't go back to Jack just now."

"I don't intend to—at least until I can get my head straightened out. There's a nice motel in New Milford—the River View. I'm going there and . . . well, try to think. What else can I do?"

He got up and walked to the window. Looking out past the peaceful campus to Rock Mountain, he said, "Right now, I don't know. But I'll try to think of something."

It occurred to her he didn't sound too helpful, but perhaps she was hoping for too much.

2

She knew she was avoiding responsibility by running away and she felt ashamed, but what *was* her responsibility? She had cashed a check for two hundred dollars at the package store and, as she drove down Shandy's peaceful main street, Raymond and his power still seemed an impossible fantasy. But it was one she now believed.

She was not particularly religious. When she thought about God at all, she thought of Him as a vague abstraction somewhere out there past Jupiter. Now she began to wonder. Star Child had denied that he and Raymond were gods or devils, but she didn't particularly trust Star Child any more, and certainly Raymond was *acting* as though he were a god. What if he *were?* What if God, enraged by millennia of war, injustice and murder, disgusted by His children's despoiling the beautiful world He had created for them, sickened by the polluted oceans and atmosphere . . . what if God had decided to send another son to earth to punish the human race by loosing a reign of love-death, torture and perversion? Perhaps what she would be waiting for in the motel was the Judgment Day. Ben, after all, had a point when he said people already killed for pleasure. They had since the beginning. Perhaps God was planning to terminate this bloody history with a final murderous orgy. Perhaps Raymond was the Recording Angel——

She told herself she had to stop. The last thing she needed was religious hysteria. She tried concentrating on her immediate needs. She had nothing with her, she'd been too afraid of seeing Jack to go home to pack. She would have to buy toothbrush, toothpaste, nightgown, clean clothes . . . Well, she could get all that in New Milford. At least it was good to get out of Shandy, away from the nightmare.

Ben's face appeared in front of her vision, moved across the windshield. The face had the same surprised expression as after she had shot him. She closed her eyes. When she opened them, the face had vanished.

For an instant, though, it had been oddly real. Not a thought or remembrance—but real.

She told herself it was nerves.

"How much for the Brie?"

"Two dollars per slice."

"Good Lord. Well, let me have it. And give me a quarter pound of coleslaw, please."

She had checked into the River View Motel overlooking the Housatonic, and then had gone into New Milford to buy the things she needed. Now she was in the A & P at the deli counter, buying lunch, for she had decided to eat as often as possible in her room. She had no idea how long she would be there, so she had to stretch her money. After waiting this long for Judgment Day, God might not be in a hurry.

The supermarket was half-empty. She saw a fat woman in Bermuda shorts, holding a baby, pushing a shopping cart down the detergent aisle. The baby reached for a bottle of Mr. Clean and the mother slapped its hand. The baby wailed. A grandmother in pink hair curlers looked disapproving.

"Anything else?" asked the counterman, putting the paper bag on the white steel countertop.

"No thanks."

She took the green bag and turned around to go to the checkout station.

Ben was standing behind her. Not a transparent ghost, but a solid, real Ben. He was clutching his chest with his left hand as his right hand reached out for her throat. As he stumbled toward her, his face full of pain and rage, she screamed and backed against the counter.

Then he was gone.

"Jesus Christ, you all right, lady?" said the counterman.

"I . . ." Control yourself, she thought. *Control.* "Yes, I'm sorry . . . I . . . I had a dizzy spell . . ."

The fat lady in Bermuda shorts was staring at her, as was the grandmother in pink hair curlers and the checkout girl and the store manager.

"You're *sure* you're all right?"

"Yes, thanks. I'm really sorry."

Clutching her green paper bag and her purse, she walked as calmly as she could to the checkout counter.

Oh God, what's happening now? she thought. What's happening *now?*

Again, she told herself it was nerves. It had to be. And guilt. She had taken Ben's life less than three hours before, and now the reaction was assaulting her. And in her state of exhaustion, the reaction was taking the form of an hallucination. It had to be that. What else could it be? Unless Raymond was now able to affect her waking mind. . . .

She rejected that. Returning to the motel with her purchases, she borrowed a fork, spoon and paring knife from Mr. Szymanowski, the friendly "pa" of the "ma and pa" hotel-management team, and went to her cabin for lunch. The room was depressingly motel modern in decor, but it was clean and the view of the river out the back window was pleasant. She turned on the TV, sat down on the comfortable bed and took out her plastic container of cole slaw and the slice of Brie, which she put on the maple bed table. She cut a wedge of the cheese with the sharp paring knife. It was ripe and good. She began on the coleslaw as *Shanghai Express* began unreeling on the "Midday Movie."

Old movies. Jack loved old movies . . . Jack was now a killer.

She forced Jack out of her mind as she watched Marlene Dietrich, languid in her black feathers, make her way through Hollywood's 1932 version of the Peking Railroad Station. Time. Time had taken on a strange new dimension in the twentieth century. Now the past was mingled with the present in the form of the thousands of old movies that continually unreeled on the millions of TV sets around the world. The Thirties lived in the Seventies. The past recaptured. Time.

(Was time to come to an end soon?)

She felt her mind assaulted by a wave of drowsiness. That was odd. She was tired, but she didn't feel sleepy. She blinked her eyes and took a deep breath to clear her head. Then she continued eating, and wondered if she could borrow some coffee from Mr. Szymanowski.

"It took more then *one* man to make me Shanghai Lily," murmured Dietrich to Clive Brooks as they leaned out the windows of the Peking–Shanghai Express, and it was forty years in the past again. Star Child's thought projection. Movies were a kind of thought projection too—so was television. It seemed obvious, but yet she'd never thought of them that way. That's what they were though: projections of the fantasies of the writers and directors, the invisible puppetmasters of the entertainment media, who sent their inner visions across vast distances (and, in the case of *Shanghai Express*, across vast reaches of time as well) to, in a way, invade the mind of the audience. The way Raymond had invaded hers. . . . She remembered the sensation of being in a movie during the graveyard dream. The dreams had been like movie scenes—horror-movie scenes.

Perhaps Norton had stumbled on the truth when he suggested that a superior civilization might have learned how to eliminate the mechanical paraphernalia of radio, telephones and television and send out a kind of continuous broadcasting on a direct, mind-to-mind "network." It was a funny idea—maybe the ultimate absurdity of the television society—except that it had unfunny overtones. If violence in television and films could affect the minds of the audience, and Helen believed it did, how much more could thought projection affect the mind? Obviously—considering what had happened to Ben and Jack—enormously.

Again, the drowsiness hit her. She found her eyelids were leaden, and she could barely sit up. Putting the coleslaw on the bed table, she lay down on the pillow, more than half asleep. She knew something was wrong. She had never been hit by drowsiness this way before: she was more fainting than growing sleepy. It was like the rush of a drug.

The last thought she had before plunging into sleep was that her mind was being anesthetized.

By Raymond. Naturally.

The bed seemed a mile wide—actually it was ten feet. She lay in the middle of it, dressed in a soft, white nightgown, caressed by cool, white-satin sheets. She felt sinfully comfortable, luxurious, blissful. She was in a totally white room empty of any furnishing or decoration except the bed. The walls, floor and ceiling were of white marble. Light emanated from nowhere and everywhere. It was pristinely beautiful, a windowless room in an enchanted castle.

There was one entrance: an arch in the wall opposite the bed that opened onto a small anteroom. She couldn't see much of the anteroom because it was plunged in a brown penumbra, but it too seemed empty. Someone must have been in it, though, because she heard a flute playing a soft melody, like a shepherd's pipe. The music relaxed her even further. She sank into the satin sheets and smiled.

Magically, there now appeared at the foot of the bed a seven-foot-high mirror. She sat up to look at it.

Forgetting her curiosity, she began admiring her reflection. How white her arms were, how beautiful her breasts. And her face! She had never looked so beautiful, she told herself. She was not a particularly vain woman, and usually she considered herself anything but a beauty. But now, in the white nightgown, sitting in the white bed, she found herself ravishing.

She smiled with pure pleasure, and the mirror smiled back.

Suddenly the face of the mirror was clouded with swirling green smoke. Magic mirror! As she watched, the smoke coiled and began to dissipate.

Her own reflection was replaced with that of a haggish woman in her eighties. She wore the same white nightgown as Helen, but it now was spotted with age. The firm flesh of her arms had become wrinkled hamhocks, her soft breasts were pendulous teats, her chestnut hair turned stringy white, her face that of a crone. She stared at the image with numb horror, realizing that the ancient woman was meant to be her. Then, again, the green smoke obscured the reflection. This time when the smoke cleared she saw a skeleton sitting in the white bed staring back at her. The nightgown was now in rotting tatters, which hung from the bones like pathetic banners.

The skeleton, she knew, was *herself*. She was looking into the future. Her future. She was observing her own corpse.

Now the room filled with the odor of apple blossoms. It was almost overpowering. She felt herself lifted gently up off the bed. To her amazement, the room's center of gravity began shifting so that she was no longer floating in front of the mirror but rather over it, looking down at the reflected skeleton that was now below her. Suddenly a blast of wind threw her down toward her own future reflection. She felt herself hurtling toward the glass. She threw up her hands to protect her face as she hit the glass, which burst into a million fragments, and found herself plunging down through the green smoke. Down, down through endless miles of nothing, twisting gently through the smoke which neither hurt her lungs nor smelled like smoke. Oddly, it smelled like apple blossoms. She remembered the apple tree in the valley of Star Child, and wondered if he was somehow trying to contact her.

Suddenly, she found herself in a cage.

It was a big cage, almost ten feet high and fifteen feet square, and it rested on the metal floor of a metal room. It was the only thing in the room, which had no windows and only one metal door. The cage was filled with men and women—a dozen or so, she judged—all of whom were black. They who were all young, all physically attractive, and all had a thin band of steel around their necks that looked to Helen like some form of identification tag. Most of them were sitting on the floor, though a few of the men leaned against the bars of the cage. Both men and women wore short, unisex gray tunics and nothing else.

"Where am I?" she asked.

No one paid any attention. She was standing in the middle of the cage next to a woman who was sitting on the floor idly cleaning her left fingernails with her right thumbnail.

"Who are you?" asked Helen, kneeling beside the woman. "What is this place?"

No answer.

Helen reached out to touch the woman's arm. To her amazement, her hand went through the flesh. She stood up, taking another look around her as she began to realize that she was invisible to the others—unseen and unheard.

She was a ghost.

The metal door of the metal room opened inward, and a white man, in a white tunic, came in, followed by three other whites in orange tunics. Unlike the blacks in the cage, who were all barefoot, the white men wore white sandals. The first man, who was carrying a clipboard under his arm and a short white stick that appeared to be some sort of club in his hand, came up to the cage and banged the stick against the bars. "Prisoners stand up," he called. As the blacks silently got to their feet, Helen went to the front of the cage and poked her fingers in the guard's eyes. Nothing. She gave up and proceeded to watch the three men in orange tunics who had come to the cage and were looking over the men and women inside. The orangies, as she thought of them, were in their thirties, and they looked a bit self-conscious, like middle executives on the make. One of them, an extremely tall man with a ski-jump nose and cruel little pig eyes, struck her as particularly in love with himself. She disliked him immediately.

"This is the new group, transferred just this morning from the Corrective Labor Facility at Attica," said the guard to the orangies. "They're the pick of the crop," he added, rather proudly.

"Yes, very good-looking," said the first orangie, a plump blond man with a cherubic, pleasant face. "*Very* good-looking."

He was eyeing one of the men, a handsome black youth. Helen became aware of something strange: none of the prisoners seemed angry or defiant. In fact, they all looked totally bored, as if they had no interest in what was happening to them.

"Come here," said the plump man, pointing to the black. He obediently stepped up to the bars. The orangie reached through and ran his hand over the black's bare arm.

"Nice. Strong. What's he in for?"

"Murder," said the guard, checking his clipboard.

"Interesting."

"He's been reconditioned, of course," continued the guard. "He's safe."

"Well, I'd *hope* so. I'll take him."

"Yes sir. His name's Ralph."

"Hello, Ralph."

"You," said the tall man with the pig eyes, pointing to the woman Helen had tried to communicate with. "Come here."

The woman stepped up to the bars, continuing to clean her nails. The tall man reached his hand through the bars and felt the woman's breast.

"Lovely," he murmured, like an oenophile sipping a vintage La Tâche. "What's her name?"

"Elaine," said the guard, checking the clipboard. "She's in for shoplifting."

"What did she get?"

"Life."

"We'll give her a parole. I'll take her."

"Yes sir."

The third orangie, a short, balding man with thick eyeglasses who looked pale as an accountant, pointed to a girl who couldn't have been older than fifteen.

"What about this one?" he asked the guard, who looked again at the clipboard.

"Her name's Lucille, Vagrancy and drunkenness. Sixty years, no parole."

"Hello, Lucille," said the accountant, making a face like a degenerate Elk. "I'll take her. I don't suppose she's a virgin?"

"No sir."

"I'll take her anyway."

"Yes sir."

"When can we have them?" asked the plump one, whose eyes were on his lover.

"We'll have them bathed and in the Coupling Rooms in half an hour, sir. Meanwhile, you can be choosing your instruments."

"Excellent."

The men started out of the room as the prisoners began sitting down. The two women and the man who had been selected remained standing.

"We got a new shipment of whips this week," said the guard, respectfully holding the door.

"How about the electric dildoes?" asked one of them. "Got them all charged up?"

"Yes sir, the dildoes are all ready," said the guard, closing the door behind him as he followed the orange tunics out of the room. By now, the blacks were mostly seated again.

"Why didn't you *say* something?" Helen said to the prisoners. "Why didn't you tell them to go to hell?"

No one heard and no one answered.

She found herself back in the green smoke, hurtling through space.

Her mind was twirling like her body now. What was *that* supposed to be? Who were the prisoners, where was the cage, who were the men in the orange tunics? Obviously, they were choosing sexual partners to take to the "Coupling Rooms," but why was she being shown this weird ceremony? And Attica? Were the blacks supposed to be convicts from the notorious New York prison?

She had no answers, only questions. And then she found herself back in the huge white bed in the white marble room, and through the door the shepherd's pipe was still playing its soft, sinuous melody.

She sat up, looking through the arch into the shadowed room beyond. Something was in the room, and she determined to see what it was. Getting out of the bed, she walked across the cold marble floor to the arch. The room was murky, bathed in a brownish light that seemed so thick it was almost sliceable. She went through the door, trying to adjust her eyes to the penumbra.

It was a large room, its walls bare and cold. The floor was made of stone, and in the center of the room a small fire was burning. Standing by the fire was a figure wearing a brown cloak that covered its entire body and a hood that covered its head and concealed its face. As she entered the room, it turned its hidden face toward her. Its silence and anonymity reminded her of the masked figure in the graveyard.

The shepherd's piping died away, and suddenly the room was filled with the soft opening strains of the "Liebestod" from *Tristan*. Helen, no Wagner fan, nevertheless recognized the gorgeous music. The Love-Death. She backed toward the arch to return to the marble room, but she bumped into something solid. Turning, she saw that the entrance had been sealed by a thick door. Now, beginning to panic, she looked for the doorknob. There was none. She tried to push the door open: it wouldn't move. She was locked in the room with the figure.

She turned back to see that it had started toward her.

"Are *you* Raymond?" she asked softly.

The figure lowered the hood, and she saw the golden hair of Ben Scovill.

"I have forgiven you," Ben said as he continued toward her. "And Raymond has forgiven you. You have killed. You are now one of us."

She said nothing, watching with apprehension as the figure came closer. She knew it could turn into anything. She remembered the decomposed body of her husband in the graveyard dream and wondered what loathsome vision would be revealed when this one opened its cloak.

But it didn't open it.

"I love you," it said tenderly.

"Don't be absurd."

"I do. I loved you in life, and I love you even more in death."

"You loved my husband," she snapped.

The figure opened its arms.

"I love all humanity, male or female."

"That's convenient."

"That is one of the teachings of Raymond," continued the figure, which was now less then five feet from her. She was pressed against the door.

"I *hate* Raymond," she exclaimed, with sudden fire. "Whatever he is, he's evil. . . . He doesn't teach love, he teaches violence."

"Violence is an expression of love."

"Bull. And don't come any closer. . . ."

"Don't you desire me? I desire you."

She said nothing, staring at his hands as they reached out to touch her. She didn't want to be touched; she was certain the fingers would somehow be repulsive. And yet when they touched her cheek there was no pain, no revulsion, but rather a surprising tenderness.

"You mustn't be afraid of me," the figure said as the music vied with the brown half-light to fill the room. "We must never be afraid of love, in life or in death."

"Ben, what do you *want?*"

"You," the figure said as it brought its mouth up to hers. Their lips brushed gently, and she felt its arms around her.

"Love is the most important thing," it whispered. "Love and sex and death. These are the foundation of life. You showed your love for me by killing me."

"That's ridiculous," she said, her eyes closed, her body responding to the caresses despite her fear.

"It's a paradox, but Raymond says truth is always a paradox."

"Who is Raymond?" she sighed as his lips kissed her ear, her cheek, her neck.

"God."

"I don't believe it."

"You will. Soon."

Suddenly, the door behind her had vanished as quickly and quietly as it had appeared, and he was leading her back to the white room. Then, as the "Liebestod" continued to pour from the other room, they were both on the satin sheets and he was taking off her nightgown and they were both naked and he was making delicate yet—paradoxically—violent love to her, kissing her skin, sucking her nipples with astounding expertise, seeming to touch every nerve in her body and flooding her with a sensuous itch as maddeningly beautiful as the sensuously itchy music that was washing over them. He was no longer a phantom-figure, no longer Raymond-Ben, no longer an object of fear or loathing, but rather her ideal lover, her beautiful lover who was lifting her to a plateau of sensuality she had never before imagined. As she lay in his arms, her eyes half-open, her ears and nose bombarded by the assault of the music and the now-faint odor of apple blossoms, her eyes became a new gateway to sensual gratification as the soft white light of the room began changing hues, turning now pink, now yellow, pale orange, blue, scarlet, purple . . .

"Ben, Ben," she began.

"Do you love me?"

"Yes, oh, God, *yes* . . ."

And at that moment she did.

"Is it more than love?"

"Yes . . ."

"Love-sex?"

"Yes . . ."

"Love-death?"

"I don't know . . ."

"Love-sex-death?"

"I don't know, I don't know . . ."

She felt something cold, hard and smooth push into her and she sucked in her breath.

"There is only one god," he whispered.

"There is only one god," she repeated.

"And his name is Raymond . . ."

"No."

Suddenly the cold thing inside her gave out an agonizing charge of electricity. She screamed and tried to push him off, but he held her down.

"Say it!" he said over the music, which was now almost deafening. "Say, 'And his name is Raymond.' . . ."

"No"—wrestling with him—"Raymond is false, he's evil . . ."

Another charge of electricity, this one more intense, filling her with a pain almost unendurable. She screamed as the room turned red and the music roared.

"*Say* it! Say there is no other god but Raymond."

"There is no other god but Raymond . . ."

She didn't care any more. As she said it, the music was replaced with a hollow, echoing laugh, and Ben vanished. The light turned white, all was still. She lay on the bed crying as she held her hands over herself, trying to soothe the burning.

An electric dildo? How hideous, she thought. How disgusting.

When she woke up in her motel bed, she noticed that *Shanghai Express* was scarcely one reel further along. She had had the three dreams in less than twenty minutes.

The second dream, the one in the cage with the black prisoners, totally baffled her. She had no idea what it was supposed to mean.

But it was the third dream that still screamed in the corners of her mind. And the curious thing was that even now, when she was awake, she could still feel the tremors of pain deep in her womb.

She decided it was a mistake to run away.

It was obvious there was no escape from the dreams: they would follow her everywhere, taunting and torturing her, making sleep, and now waking, to be dreaded. She must act. There might be nothing she could do against the apparently supernatural powers of Raymond–Star Child (assuming they were two parts of the same), but she could at least report the murders and turn herself in to the police.

She checked out of the motel, to the confusion of Mr. Szymanowski, and drove to West Redding, where the nearest state police barracks was located. Parking in front of the neat white building, she went inside. Sergeant Seth Bixby, a big, pleasant-faced redhead, looked up from behind his desk. "Good morning," he said. "Can I help you?"

"Yes. My name is Helen Bradford, and I've just committed a murder. Here's the weapon." She pulled the Smith & Wesson from her purse and placed it on the desk. The sergeant looked at it. She thought he was remarkably calm.

"Who did you murder, Mrs. Bradford?"

"A young man named Ben Scovill. He attacked me, and I shot him."

"Self-defense?"

"Yes."

"Well, I think, before you say anything else, you should get yourself a lawyer. I have to warn you that anything you say may be used against you in a court of law. . . ."

"Oh God," she interrupted, "forget all that! I'm admitting I killed him, but *he* was a murderer. There are three bodies buried in his cellar—all you have to do is go look! And my husband's one of them."

"One of the bodies?"

"No. I mean one of the *murderers*. He and Ben killed a hitchhiker. Oh, I know it sounds insane, but *they're* insane. Their minds have been taken over by . . ." she stopped. No, don't say it. He's already looking at me like I'm a prime nut case. Don't say it. ". . . by an alien force."

"An alien force." He took the gun and checked the chambers. "How many shots did you fire?"

"Three."

"That's interesting. There are six bullets in the gun."

He clicked the chambers for her inspection, and it was true: the gun was fully loaded. She stared at him.

"But that's impossible. I remember: I fired three shots, and I've had the gun with me ever since . . . unless . . ." Was it *possible?* Could Jack somehow have found out what had happened and then followed her to the motel and broken into her room while she was asleep and reloaded the gun? But why? Why go to such incredible lengths, unless he was afraid she *might* go to the police, and this was his way to discredit her, make her look foolish, hysterical . . . even mad . . . ?

"Unless what, Mrs. Bradford?" asked the trooper.

"My husband must have reloaded it at the motel so you wouldn't believe me."

"Does that seem likely?"

"It's not *likely,* but murder isn't likely either. I'm telling you: I fired the gun three times and the bodies are in the cellar. If you want proof, let's go to the house and look."

"All right." He stood up. "I'll get some help and we can get started."

"You know, I'm not drunk and I'm really not crazy."

He looked at her but said nothing. Then he opened the door to the rear of the barracks and called in, "Highet and Rydell? Turn off the boob tube. We've got a job."

It took the three troopers two hours to dig up the entire cellar floor, but by five-thirty they had found nothing.

Helen, who was sitting on the blanket chest (which had been emptied of all the "props"), watched in silence as Sergeant Bixby came over to her, wiping his forehead with a handkerchief.

"Mrs. Bradford, I'd hate to think this is some practical joke. You know this has taken a lot of our time and a lot of the taxpayers' money."

"He took the bodies away," she said quietly.

"Who?"

"Jack. My husband. He came here and found Ben

and knew something had gone wrong. He must have dug the bodies up and buried them somewhere else."

"All by himself? When it's taken me and Highet and Rydell two hours to dig up this floor?"

"He knew where they were."

"Of course. I hadn't thought of that. And then he found you, took your gun away, and filled the empty chambers. . . ."

"Look, I *know* you don't believe me, but isn't there a woman from Fairfax named Betty Fredericks who's missing?"

For a moment the skepticism left his face. "Yes."

"And the Siebert girl from Shandy? You haven't found her yet, have you?"

"No."

"Those are two of them, and the third one's a hitchhiker named Roger."

"Uh huh. And how about Judge Crater?"

"I'm trying to help you. . . ."

"Look, Mrs. Bradford, you read about the Fredericks woman's disappearance in the paper. . . ."

"No!"

"And you knew the Siebert girl ran away . . ."

"She didn't run away, she was murdered! It was something they call a love-death. . . . This place is a chapel, that box over there *used* to have a shawl and candlestick on it because it was the altar—"

"An *altar?*"

"Oh God, I *know* it sounds nuts, but it's the truth. Believe me, it's the truth. I killed Ben Scovill, Ben killed the two women, my husband killed the hitchhiker, and something called Raymond is coming to . . ."

She watched him watch her.

"You think it's a joke, don't you? Violence is love. Love-death is beautiful. There's only one god and his name is Raymond. Oh God, it's wonderful!"

She was now laughing and crying at the same time.

She buried her face in her hands. The sergeant came over and patted her back.

"That's all right, Mrs. Bradford. You're the third person who's told us you murdered the Fredericks woman."

"No, I killed Ben . . ."

"Oh yes, I forgot. Anyway, it's all right. We'll take you home now."

"*Home?*" She looked up, her eyes red from crying. "I have no home any more." She thought a moment, then said, "Let's go down to the campus. You can talk to Dr. Akroyd. He's the school psychiatrist and he'll tell you I'm telling the truth. He knows everything. Well, almost everything—"

"How?"

"I told him. I wondered if I were crazy, so I went to him."

The sergeant nodded to the other troopers.

"All right, Mrs. Bradford, let's go down to the campus."

They found Norton playing tennis with Jeremy Bernstein, while at the next court Lyman Henderson was playing his wife, Marjorie. How peaceful it all looked, she reflected, as she parked her car behind the two police cars. How absurdly peaceful. Didn't they know they were surrounded by murder and madness? Didn't they know something horribly frightening was coming? Well, she would tell them. Everything. If nothing else, she would alert everyone to the danger— and Norton would back her up.

She got out of the car as the troopers got out of theirs. The four players had stopped and were watching now, surprised by the appearance of the patrol cars on the near-empty, peaceful campus. "There he is," said Helen to the sergeant, pointing at Norton, and they walked across the grass to the court.

"Dr. Akroyd," said Sergeant Bixby, "we want to ask you a few questions."

"Of course," said Norton, leaning his racquet against the net-post. Lyman and Marjorie Henderson were coming, too, as was Jeremy Bernstein.

"Norton," Helen said, "I decided I was wrong. I've told the police. They don't believe me, which isn't much of a surprise, but I think they have to be convinced. Would you please tell them about the . . . dreams?"

He looked at the tall, red-headed sergeant, then back at Helen. "But I thought we agreed not to—"

She gestured impatiently.

"I know. I said I was wrong. The police should know—if for no other reason than to stop Jack from killing someone else."

Lyman Henderson looked astounded. "Jack *killed* someone?"

Norton shook his head. "No. Helen's been having some unusual dreams, and she's come to me for treatment. Officer," he said to Bixby, "I think it would be better if we discussed this in my office."

"Norton, I told you . . ."

"Helen, you're fantasizing."

"It's not a fantasy, dammit, it's fact!"

And then she began to understand. Of course, how stupid of her. Either Norton was causing the dreams—through hypnosis or some sort of advanced mental telepathy—and had been leading her on all along. Or Norton was being taken over, too, was having the dreams himself, had become one of them. . . . That was how Ben had known she had gone to his house that morning—Norton had told him. And then, after she had shot Ben, she had gone directly to Norton and told him. That's why he hadn't urged her to go to the police; but, afraid that she might, he had followed her to the motel and reloaded her gun while Jack went to the cellar and moved the bodies. They had to discredit her, make her seem mad. . . . She had to be careful. They could commit her to an asylum for life. She had heard of cases like that, and Jack certainly wouldn't lift a finger to help her. Maybe the whole business was a scheme to drive her mad, or make her *appear* mad, so nobody would believe her when she told the truth. . . . She had to be careful. Very careful.

She turned to Sergeant Bixby.

"I'm sorry," she said. "Dr. Akroyd's right. I've been under a strain lately, and I've been having these . . ." She put her hand on her forehead to dramatize her weariness. ". . . these dreams. I'm terribly sorry I caused all this trouble."

The trooper looked at Norton, who said, "Take her home. She'll be all right. I'll assume full responsibility."

Sergeant Bixby shrugged and took Helen's arm. As the others watched, they started across the lawn to the parked cars, and Lyman Henderson said to Norton in a low voice, "How sick *is* Helen?"

"Very."

"What would make her think Jack had killed someone?"

"She's experiencing some form of persecution fantasies. I'm afraid she thinks Jack wants to kill *her*."

Lyman considered this, then looked at the psychiatrist.

"But Jack accused *you* of doing something to his mind. Is he having persecution fantasies too?"

"Possibly," said Norton. "Jack hasn't come to me for treatment yet, as Helen has, but, according to her, his drinking has caused a real problem in their marriage. I hope I'll be able to help them, but of course one never knows—" He turned to Jeremy. "How about another game?"

They returned to the tennis court as Lyman watched the patrol cars pull away from the curb.

Driving home, followed by the two police cars, she tried to fit the new piece into the jigsaw. First Ben and Jack; now Norton. It was spreading. Slowly she was being surrounded by Raymonds. If Raymond were actually Norton, it would in a way be easier to understand. But if Raymond were some kind of unknown force, why would he take over Norton's mind? Unless it was because he knew she had told Norton about the dreams—which he would know, because when he was in her mind he could see all her thoughts. The moment she told Norton, Raymond took over his mind, converting him into another apostle who would make the pilgrimage to the top of Rock Mountain to await the arrival of the new God . . . the twelve apostles, or maybe the twenty-eight, or perhaps the two thousand. She envisioned the whole world prostrating itself to the new deity, called to prayer by the ultimate muezzin, Thought Projection. Insane. And yet, it wasn't quite that simple. While it was true the power of Raymond to project his thoughts seemed no longer to be limited to the top of Rock Mountain . . . he had, after all, reached her as far as New Milford, and he was now able to reach Norton . . . still it didn't seem that he had tried to reach anyone farther away—as in New York or London. Wherever he was, the mechanism that generated the electromagnetic field that carried his thoughts apparently was limited. If that weren't true, why was he wasting his time with nonentities such as herself? If he wanted to be worshiped as a god why not recruit from the majors—the President or the Pope or Mao Tse-Tung? If one of *them* should announce the arrival of a new god on earth, the whole world would know and tend to accept. So Raymond's power must still be limited to Shandy. What kind of a god was that?

She turned into her driveway and drove up to the garage. Jack, sitting on the front lawn, got up when he saw the two police cars. They parked in front of the house and the sergeant got out. He walked across the grass to Jack.

"Are you Mr. Bradford?"

"Yes. Anything wrong?" He was watching Helen get out of her car.

"Do you know Ben Scovill?" asked Sergeant Bixby.

"Of course. He lives on the other side of the mountain."

The trooper hesitated tactfully. "Mr. Bradford, we know your wife's been under a strain lately. Can you tell me anything about the dreams she's been having?"

"Apparently something that calls itself 'Raymond'—I think that's the name—has been appearing in her dreams and telling her he's coming to Earth, or something like that. It's shaken her up enough to see a psychiatrist. But what's that got to do with Ben?"

"Your wife told us she killed him."

"What?"

"And that you'd murdered a hitchhiker."

"Me?"

"Look, Mr. Bradford, we've talked to Mr. Akroyd, and I understand your wife's got a slight problem. We checked out the Scovill house and there's nothing there, so we brought her home. Oh, by the way, she gave me this gun—" He handed the Smith & Wesson to Jack. "It *is* hers?"

"It's ours. It's registered."

"I'd suggest you keep it away from her. In her present state of mind it's possible she might try to harm herself—or you. I wouldn't get too worried, but an ounce of prevention . . ."

"I understand. And sergeant, I hope she . . . we didn't cause you too much trouble."

Sergeant Bixby grinned slightly. "Oh, I enjoy digging up basements."

When they were gone, Helen came across the lawn to her husband. She looked at the gun.

"Are you going to keep that?"

"That's right."

She looked at him. "Where did you put Ben's body?"

"You really should try to control your imagination, Helen. You could get me, and yourself, in a lot of trouble."

"So we're still playing games?"

"Is it a game?"

"You know it is."

"I take it you've come home to stay?"

"Yes. I'm not afraid of you any more."

"Afraid?" He put his hand on her cheek. "Why in the world would you be afraid of me?"

"Did you and Ben really make love?"

He lowered his hand.

"I bought a nice steak for dinner. Should I put it on?"

Giving up, she nodded wearily. He started toward the house but hadn't gone more than a few steps when he stopped and turned around again.

"By the way, I forgot to say 'welcome home.'" He smiled pleasantly and started back toward the house, carrying the gun lovingly in his right hand.

PART IV

Revelations

1

They ate dinner in the terrible silence of lost trust. Occasionally, casual remarks were made on antiseptic topics, as if by mutual unspoken agreement they were going to keep up the façade of normality through habit if nothing else. But it was a charade and she was relieved when the agonizing meal was over and she could go upstairs. After removing her clothes, she proceeded to take a long bath. Submerged to her neck in the hot water and pink Vitabath, she tried to relax, which under the circumstances was rather difficult. She told herself at least he wouldn't dare try to kill her for a while. The police had been there, they had heard her story and even though they didn't believe it they would remember it. If she vanished or died now, certainly they would be suspicious at the very least. So for the time being she was relatively safe.

She hoped.

Stepping out of the tub, she dried herself, then brushed her teeth. As she was putting on a nightgown, she heard voices downstairs. Quietly she opened the bathroom door and tiptoed down the hall to the head of the stairs. She recognized the voice of Jeremy Bernstein. While it was not unusual for Jeremy to drop by unannounced to have a glass of wine and "shoot the English department shit," as he put it, still, tonight it was a little too pat to think his visit was coincidental.

Was Jeremy, too, one of them?

They were talking softly, furtively.

"I always wanted to believe in something, even when I was a kid," Jeremy was saying, "but I was always too damned skeptical."

"I was the same," replied Jack. "They always told me, 'Believe. Have faith.' But I always wanted facts. . . ."

She moved nearer the stairs to hear better, and stepped on a squeaky board. Damn, she thought, as the conversation downstairs stopped. Silence. They knew she was listening. The Great Theological Debate was not meant for her ears (how many Raymonds can dance on the head of a pin?). She went back to the bedroom—her bedroom now, not his-and-hers: he had told her he was going to sleep across the hall. She turned out the light and went to the north window to look up at the mountain. It was another clear night, and there was enough moon now to see the top. There, behind the protective screen of pines, was the clearing Ben had made. Above it the stars twinkled in their silence. Was that silence about to be broken?

They obviously thought so, those two downstairs.

She went to her bed. The bath had relaxed her, but she wasn't sleepy. Sleep had become fearful; the night was her enemy. But the day was becoming her enemy too—the sunlight as deceptive as the dark. Reality was becoming iridescent: one moment she would see someone in one color, and then, abruptly, the color would change. One moment Norton was her helper and friend, the next her enemy. And now Jeremy too? She had no more anchor, no more roots. Despite her remark to Norton at the tennis court, fact and fantasy were beginning to merge in her mind, and her inability to differentiate between them was becoming as frightening to her as her fear of Jack. And, most maddening, she still couldn't see a thread of logic to what was happening, unless she accepted the premise that Norton somehow was causing it all to prove his theory (which seemed sadly illogical) or that Raymond was gathering an army of apostles to herald his arrival on earth (which seemed insane). Perhaps she deserved those knowing looks the troopers had exchanged among themselves and with Jack when they were talking about her. She didn't *think* she deserved them . . . and she'd always heard that, if you worried about your sanity, that meant you were actually sane. God knew, though, she was worried. . . .

To distract herself from such nervous thoughts, she turned the bedlight on and looked under the bed table for something to read. *New York Magazine, Vogue, The National Geographic*—what a hodgepodge her reading habits were, she reflected—three paperback mysteries (two of which she had read), *Smithsonian, Newsweek, Paris-Match* . . . all out of date, all read. She got out of bed, crossed the room to the 1920s-style bookshelf they had found the previous year at a tag sale and ran her finger over the paperback spines that filled it. More mysteries, gothics, *The Best and the Brightest, Three Plays* by Chekhov, *The Nine Tailors, Eyeless in Gaza, La Chartreuse du Parme,* old friends that seemed all the more faithful and loyal now that her human ones were proving so faithless. She selected the Stendhal and returned to bed, deciding that a total escape into another century was what she needed. But she couldn't concentrate on the book, as familiar and well loved as it was. Her mind kept reverting to the dreams, most particularly to the dream of the cage with the prisoners and the orangies. That stood out from all the other dreams. In the others she had always been present, an actor in the horror-playlets, the victim, actually, being worked on by Raymond in his various disguises. But in this cage dream she had been an observer, a ghost. Nor was that dream a horror-playlet like the others with their Gothic-surrealist settings and their perhaps crude but nonetheless effective atmospheres of terror and death. The cage dream had seemed real, in an unreal way. She felt she had witnessed something that had actually happened, rather than the projections of a nightmare mentality. But where had it happened and who were the people supposed to be? And why was that dream alone so different?

She remembered the strong odor of the apple blossoms she had smelled just before the dream, and again she thought of Star Child. He had seemed to vanish from her dreams, as if he had been chased away by Raymond. Was Star Child battling Raymond for possession of her mind, and was the cage dream his way of telling her something about himself and Raymond?

She heard the front door close and, a moment later, a car starting. That would be Jeremy Bernstein leaving. She was again alone with Jack in the house. Acting on an impulse, she got out of bed and went to the door to bolt it. Then, feeling better, she returned to the bed and tried again to immerse herself in the novel.

She heard Jack coming up the stairs, the wooden steps squeaking in the places they always squeaked. She had heard the same sounds hundreds of times, but whereas previously they had always been friendly noises (Jack coming up to join her in bed), now they seemed menacing because Jack had become menacing. Squeak, squeak. The rats in the chapel.

He reached the upstairs and slowly walked down the hall to her door, where he stopped. Not in front of *his* door, across the hall, but in front of *her* door. For a moment she hoped he was going to knock and ask to come in and talk to her, perhaps explain everything away, perhaps restore the past. Maybe she was wrong about him, maybe the whole thing *was* in her imagination: Raymond, Star Child, Ben . . . Ben. She hadn't imagined Ben, nor had she imagined killing him.

Her hope vanished, replaced by apprehension. Why was he standing out there? She looked at the door, at the lock. It was a sturdy wooden door, and the bolt was brass. Still, he could break it in. But he wouldn't, he *wouldn't*. He couldn't be that crazy, not with the police having been there only hours before. . . .

But why was he standing there?

"Jack?" she called, softly.

Silence.

"Jack, is that you?"

Stupid, who else could it be?

Silence.

Suddenly she was furious. All her resentment and anxiety burst loose. She threw back her sheet, got out of the bed, went to the door and pushed open the bolt.

"Goddamit, Jack I've had *enough*," she said, throwing open the door.

Her voice ricocheted around the room. A blast of wind roared through the open door past the monstrous thing that was standing outside. She stepped back, literally reeling. It was a tall . . . man? She supposed it was a man, or *had* been. . . . Its face was green, the skin bulging with sores, the mouth gaping wide in a silent scream, the teeth yellowed fangs, the eyes manic. It wore nothing but a tattered rag around its loins and its body was like the decomposed body in the graveyard dream. Except this wasn't a dream. It was real, standing outside her door, staring at her with those ghastly eyes, eyes that had surely seen the ultimate blasphemies of the universe. As she stared back at it, it lurched through the door, raising its long arms and stretching its enormous fingers to touch her.

She ran to the corner of the room as it lunged toward her, a gigantic, grotesque wind-up doll. Her back against the corner, she watched it come toward her, its hand reaching for her throat. As she felt it touch her, her vision blacked out and she lost consciousness.

He was pleasant looking, slightly beefy, early thirties, she judged, and he'd been sitting at the bar for over an hour drinking beer. He was wearing plaid Bermuda shorts and white gym socks and loafers. It was a roadhouse on Route 6, near the state border. A neon Schaefer Beer sign glorified the window. Above the door the Fedders air conditioner rumbled monotonously, competing with the soundtrack of a 1957 "I Love Lucy" rerun on the TV above the bar. Two men, half drunk, battled endlessly with a pinball machine in the corner. Sam, the roadhouse owner, leaned at the end of the bar talking to an overweight woman with a beehive hairdo who was drinking straight Bourbon on the rocks.

The young couple in the booth had come in about twenty minutes before ten and started drinking gin and tonic. They had specified Schweppes.

Now the woman got out of the booth and came over to Bermuda Shorts.

"Hello," she said.

He looked at her. She was attractive: sharp, intelligent features, short black hair, a good figure that was perhaps too thin. She was wearing Lily Pulitzer pants (Bermuda Shorts didn't know this) and a white silk blouse. A classy dame, he thought as he looked at her.

"Hello," he replied.

"My husband and I thought you might like to join us."

Cool as the Fedders. He looked over at the booth where the man with the beard nodded pleasantly. What the hell is *this?* . . .

"Well, maybe," he said. "Yeah, why not?"

She returned to the booth. He picked up his beer and followed her. The Beard stood up and extended his hand.

"My name's Jeremy," he said.

"Hello. I'm Doug."

"Glad to meet you, Doug."

"I'm Marcia," said the woman, sliding in the booth and indicating with a pat of her hand on the bench that Doug should sit next to her. He did.

"May we buy you a drink?" said Marcia.

Doug eyed his half-empty glass. "Why not?"

He drained his glass as Jeremy signaled to Sam for another round.

"We saw you were all alone and thought you might like some company," said Marcia. "We're alone too."

Doug looked at her, then at her smiling, bearded husband across from her. He wondered what the game was.

"Uh huh," was all he said. He'd take it slow.

"Do you live around here?" asked Jeremy.

"In Wingdale, over in York state."

"I see. Do you work at the hospital?"

"Nah. I own a rig, do long-distance hauling."

"Fascinating," said Marcia. "Your wife must miss you on those long hauls."

"She did. I guess that's why she took off with the mailman."

"You're kidding."

"No I'm not. They're shacking up in Tallahassee right now. Sent me a postcard last week. Talk about balls!"

Sam brought the new round, which Jeremy paid for, and Doug offered his new friends a Newport, which they declined. He lighted one.

"So. What do you do?" he asked, exhaling.

"I teach English in Shandy," said Jeremy.

"No shit."

"Well, there's *some.*"

"An English teacher! Goddam." He lowered his voice. "Hey, is it true Shakespeare was a faggot? Somebody told me that once."

Jeremy suppressed a laugh.

"I think he maybe made it both ways."

"No shit."

Marcia said, "Someone once told me a lot of truck-drivers are gay."

Doug looked at her. "Huh?"

Then she smiled, and he laughed. "Yeah, that's pretty good. Fairy truckdrivers." He raised his glass. "Well, here's to us."

"Right—to us."

They drank, then Doug said, "Say, I'm glad you asked me over. Tell the truth, I was sort of depressed."

"About what?"

"Oh, you know. Life. My wife taking off with the goddam postal service. Isn't that too much? I was too stupid to suspect anything, but I should have known. Christ, the kid had hair down to his navel."

"A hippie?"

"Bet your ass. Temporary job. Probably living in a field shacked up with a pig or something. Well, now he's got Madge. Same difference."

He drank from his beer.

"Are you getting a divorce?"

"Sure. Desertion."

"Any kids?"

"No, luckily. How about you two?"

"I've had two miscarriages," said Marcia.

"Oh, sorry to hear it. Going to try again?"

"No. We've decided we don't want children, after all. They're too expensive. Besides . . ." He felt her cool fingers on his left knee, lightly rubbing. ". . . they cramp one's style."

He looked at her.

"You know," she went on, softly, "I think it's this place that's depressing. Why don't you come to our house for a nightcap? Maybe that would cheer you up."

A long silence. Then he said, "What are you two, some kind of traveling Bob and Ted and Carol and Alice act?"

Jeremy leaned forward.

"You see, Doug, I've developed a heart condition that prevents me from . . . you know. And because I love my wife and want her to be happy, we've made this sort of arrangement where we go out and find her . . . company."

He digested this, slowly.

"No shit."

"You won tonight's lottery," smiled Marcia. "Interested?"

Another long silence as he looked her over.

"Why the fuck not?"

"Shakespeare," said Marcia, "couldn't have put it more elegantly."

A half hour later the two cars pulled up in front of the Bernsteins' charming house on the edge of the school campus.

"Nice place," said Doug as they walked to the front door. "I like old houses. I hate that modern shit."

"So do I," said Jeremy, unlocking the door. "Most of it's gotten so banal."

"Huh?"

"Dull. Of course, you get *some* good designs, but, with construction costs going sky high, nobody but millionaires can afford them."

"I know what you mean. I'd like to build a house, but Christ, the money! I got a trailer. It's a nice one, but it's still a trailer."

"This house belongs to the school. They rent it to us cheap."

"Hey, that's a good deal."

They went into the small entrance foyer, Jeremy turning on a lamp, then into the comfortably furnished living room with its big Oriental run. Doug looked around approvingly.

"You people done a nice job decorating. I think that's important. My wife's taste was pure shit, like everything else about her. But I like this. Really nice. That's a beautiful rug."

"Thank you."

Marcia sat down on the big white nubby sofa. An awkward silence. Doug grinned self-consciously.

"Well, what do we do?"

"Let's all relax with a drink first," suggested Jeremy. "You sticking to beer?"

"Well . . . you have any Seagram's Seven?"

"I'm afraid not. . . ."

"Okay, I'll have a beer then."

"All I've got is Tuborg."

"That'll be fine."

Jeremy went into the kitchen, leaving Marcia and Doug alone. She was watching him. He turned slightly red and looked around the room again.

"You must like it here," he said. "I mean, Shandy's a nice little town. . . ."

"I detest it," said Marcia.

"You do? Why?"

"I like New York. There's nothing here but cows."

He grinned.

"You're a real kooky dame, you know?" He lowered his voice. "You and your husband do this often?"

"You're the first."

He blinked with surprise. "The *first?*"

"Does that make a difference?"

"Well, I don't know. It's, uh . . . yeah. It *does* make a difference. Doesn't it to you?"

"Depends on how it goes."

"You don't feel . . . nervous?"

"Should I?"

"I don't know about you, but I'm shitting Ping-Pong balls."

She looked at him.

"My God, I've never heard *that* before."

He laughed, relieved to have gotten a reaction from the Ice Queen. Jeremy came back with a tray of drinks and smiled at the general hilarity.

"Someone make a funny?" he asked.

"He said . . ." She pointed at Doug, as she choked with laughter. ". . . he was shitting Ping-Pong balls! God, it's marvelous!"

"I just made it up," said Doug proudly.

"It's very original."

"Hey, professor, you think I ought to be a writer?"

"Could be." Jeremy smiled, handing him the glass of beer.

"Yeah, old Doug the author—"

"There's more money in truckdriving."

Jeremy brought his wife her tonic.

"I don't know about that," said Doug, sitting down on the opposite sofa. "There's this writer that's got a big farm near Wingdale. They say he makes a fucking fortune. Sells his books to Hollywood and the paperbacks . . ."

"He's probably a hack," said Jeremy primly. "They're not writers."

"Oh." Doug looked confused. Then, "Hey, you got any records?"

"Well . . ." Jeremy looked dubious. "Like some Bach?"

"Nah, I meant . . . you know. I thought me and Marcia could dance. You know, to warm things up."

"Oh."

"Put on the Cole Porter, darling," said Marcia. "That's nice and smooth. Like Doug."

"Yeah, old Doug's a real Fred Astaire."

"I'll bet you're a terrific dancer," said Marcia.

"I do a great frug."

Marcia rolled her eyes as she stood up.

"Not to Cole Porter. Let's just cheek to cheek. Nice and old-fashioned and sexy."

She came over to him and held out her hand as her husband searched through the albums. Doug got up, looking uncertain. Marcia smiled.

"You're uh . . ." he hesitated. "You're sure you want to do this?"

"Uh huh."

"You know, once I push the 'go' button, I don't stop easy."

"Good."

He looked past her at Jeremy. "You're sure he doesn't mind?"

"Of course not. He's happy for both of us."

"Jesus." He shook his head as "Night and Day" came from the loudspeakers. "You two are something else."

He took her in his arms and they started dancing in the middle of the room. Jeremy watched them for a while from the hi-fi. Then he turned off a lamp.

"Good idea," said Marcia. "Turn off more."

"Here we are at Roseland," said Jeremy, going around the room turning off the other lamps."

"Don't turn them *all* off," called Doug.

"Why not? It's magic time."

"You two are too goddam much."

Off went the final lamp, and now only the light from the entrance hall spilled into the room. Jeremy stood in a corner, a dark shadow among the shadows, his eyes fixed on the two figures turning slowly by the sofa.

"Getting horny?" whispered Marcia in Doug's ear.

"Yeah."

"I find you irresistible."

"No shit."

"Do you find me irresistible."

"Well, I don't feel like resisting."

"I'm crazy about sex. Aren't you?"

"Yeah, I like it. It's here to stay."

"Tell me something."

"Like what?"

"Oh, that you'd like to tear my clothes off."

"I'd like to tear your clothes off."

"And lay me right here on the rug."

"Jesus, can't we use the sofa?"

"The rug's more basic."

"We might get a spot on it, or something."

"Oh, come *on*."

She stepped away and started unbuttoning her blouse.

"Is your husband going to *watch?*"

"Why shouldn't he? We're married."

"Jesus, I don't understand you two at *all*. He's

supposed to be jealous . . ." He raised his voice, calling: "Hey, Jeremy, you really want me to lay your wife right here in the middle of the living room?"

"You'll be doing us both a favor, Doug," came the soft reply from the dark corner.

"Well, what the hell. I don't want to seem un-friendly, or anything."

He started pulling his sportshirt over his head as "Night and Day" segued into "I've Got You Under My Skin." Then he tossed the shirt on the sofa and began unbuttoning his pants. Suddenly he stopped.

"I can't do it," he said.

"What do you mean?" Marcia was down to her bra and panties and didn't look happy about roadblocks.

"Well, I just *can't*, that's all. Not with your husband standing over there watching. It's just not *natural*."

She stepped up to him and put her hands on his bare hairy chest.

"But don't you see, darling, that's half the fun of it."

"I don't believe in kinky sex. Once you start experimenting, you end up fucking ears or something."

She giggled as she pressed her body against his.

"That sounds fun. Now, come on. Don't be a poop de partie. Here, let me do your fly."

She unbuttoned his fly and pulled down his Bermuda shorts.

"Woops-ee-daisy!"

As they dropped to his feet, his "go" button was distinctly reactivated.

"Well, I don't know . . . Jeremy, can't you go in the bedroom and watch TV? It really makes me feel embarrassed, you standing there. In fact, it gives me the goddam creeps."

Silence. Then Jeremy said, "I'll go in the kitchen."

They waited as he crossed the room, then disappeared into the kitchen.

"Feel better?" said Marcia, putting her lips on his.

"Yeah."

He unhooked her bra and dropped it on the floor as she tugged down his Jockey shorts.

"Let's dance nude," she whispered.

"Okay."

She pulled off her panties, and they began dancing in the dark.

"Oh my God," he groaned.

"What's wrong?"

"I may drop my load on the rug."

"Would you stop worrying about the damned *rug?*"

"It looks expensive. . . ."

"So what?"

They slowly swayed back and forth to "I Concentrate on You," both rubbing their hands over each others' backs and bottoms. After a while he whispered, "I can't stand this much longer."

"Me either."

"Let's do it *now,* before I shoot a hole through the wall."

She took his hand and led him to the sofa, where she lay down. He eased himself on top of her.

"Glad we picked you up?" she whispered.

"Yeah."

"I like you, Doug. A lot."

"Yeah."

"Do you like me?"

"Shut up, will you? I'm about to come . . ."

"Not *yet!*"

"Oh Christ."

Heavy breathing becoming heavier. Moans. Then a wild grunt from Doug as he shot into her. The panting slowed, and they lay still.

The kitchen door opened and a shaft of light leapt across the room.

"All done?" asked Jeremy.

"Yeah, you can come in now. And thanks for going out of the room. That helped."

He heard the husband walk toward the sofa.

"You both happy?" he asked.

Doug started to sit up.

"Like a goddam lark. . . ." He stopped as he saw Jeremy's shadow projected on the wall in front of him. The shadow's arm was raised high, and its hand held something long and pointed.

Doug started to yell when he saw the long point start down. Then he felt the steel cut into his back and a terrible pain as it pierced his right lung.

"Oh Jesus . . ." he muttered, half-twisting.

The knife plunged again. And again.

The third time killed him. Marcia felt his dead weight collapse on her. She closed her eyes, feeling the warm blood on her fingers as she rubbed her hands over his back.

She whispered to Jeremy, "How did it feel?"

He didn't answer for a moment. Then, quietly: "Just as we were told."

The two people sat on the white-cushioned floor of the small room, and they both looked bored. One, the tall pig-eyed man Helen remembered from the cage dream, was actually yawning. The other, the attractive woman prisoner Helen had tried to communicate with in the same dream, was staring at her toes. Between them was a bottle of wine and two glasses.

Helen, once again a ghost, stood in the corner of the metal cubicle, watching. Again, she smelled the faint odor of apple blossoms.

Finally, the man spoke.

"You know where I'm going this afternoon?"

The woman said nothing. The man picked up his wine glass.

"If you *did* know—if anything could penetrate that dead brain of yours—*then* you might react. You might even treat me like the big hero I'm supposed to be. Anyway, I'm going to a new world—or an old one. A world where people can still feel pain and pleasure, where they still have emotions. If you had any idea what a bore you are . . ." He shook his head as he sipped the wine. "Well, it's not your fault. But God, what a send-off celebration *this* has been."

There was a knock on the metal door.

"Yes?"

The door was opened by the white-tunicked guard Helen remembered from the previous dream.

"Excuse me, Captain," said the guard, "but the Vice-President has just arrived."

"All right."

The guard looked curiously at the woman.

"You, uh . . . didn't find her satisfactory, sir? I noticed you didn't call for any equipment."

"What's the point of it? In fact, what's the point of a love-death when they can't love and they're not afraid of death? They might as well leave these people in Attica."

"Yes, sir, I know what you mean. We've been getting a lot of complaints lately."

"The whole program's become a farce. The love-death 'privilege'—what's the privilege when it's no fun? Even the wine's terrible."

"It's the last California vintage, sir, before the vine-yard-cells were discontinued. But Captain, is there anything I can do? I mean, this *is* a special occasion for you, and the Council especially wanted you to be pleased. . . ."

The man got to his feet.

"Can you find me someone who reacts?"

"You know that's against the law, sir. . . ."

"Well, then there's nothing you can do for me." His tone was irritated. He started toward the door; the guard looked at the woman, who was still sitting, staring at her toes.

"You don't want to finish her, Captain?" said the guard.

The man looked back.

"As far as I'm concerned, she's already dead," he said. Then he walked out of the room.

*   *   *

"There have been many great moments in the history of mankind," said the handsome, gray-haired woman at the podium encircled by potted palms, "but I think all of us will agree this is perhaps the most important moment in the history of our race: the moment that will decide our survival on this planet. It is, literally, our last chance."

She paused to let her words sink in, and Helen took the opportunity to assimilate her new surroundings. She was standing at the rear of a large room with a plastic dome over its center. The room had been converted into a temporary auditorium by the setting up of about fifty folding chairs on which an audience of orange-tunicked men and women were sitting listening to the speaker on the dais. Six men were seated behind the speaker, and she recognized one of them as the pig-eyed man from the previous scene. Behind the dais a ceiling-high curtain concealed the rear of the room. The woman at the podium wore a purple tunic; on the front of her lectern was fastened the circular seal of the Vice-President of the United States.

"I don't think any of us would deny," continued the Vice-President, who had a well-trained speaking voice, "that our civilization has progressed remarkably in many directions during the past several generations. Medical science has found immunizations against the diseases that killed our grandparents, diseases such as cancer and arteriosclerosis. Advanced psychotherapy has liberated us from the frustrating taboos of the past: now we of the governing class are free to satisfy our sexual appetites in any fashion we choose without the threat of antiquated social condemnation or criminal prosecution. Perhaps, most important, we have achieved a level of sociological stability that frees us from the constant class warfare that plagued the last decades of the previous century and the first decades of our own. Now, thanks to the development of thought projection, we are able to control the lower, less-stable classes by means of psychosexual nightmares: terror, which years ago titillated our forefathers in their films and television, has now become an instrument of government policy. Strikes, upheavals and revolutions are happily as extinct as the lion and the tiger. We have achieved class peace.

"So, in many ways, we live in a utopia. But while we have corrected many of the evils of the past, the past—as we are all too acutely aware—still reaches out with a dead hand that threatens the existence of our planet. I need not tell you what I'm speaking of. We have all watched it grow worse throughout our lifetimes until it has become intolerable. It is . . . the pollution."

With quiet drama she paused and looked up at the plastic dome over her head, as did most of the others in the room. And now Helen became aware of what was outside the dome. More accurately, whereas she had first assumed it was night, she now saw that the sky above the dome was not a night sky but rather a day sky in which the sun was obliterated by roiling, oily-brown clouds so thick that barely any light penetrated. It reminded her of a sky over Los Angeles when once she had sunk through the purple smog in a jet.

"We all know the story," continued the Vice-President. "How, despite the warnings of the ecologists, during the eighties and nineties of the past century our forefathers obtusely, callously, continued to burn the ever-dwindling fossil fuels while the pollution of the air and oceans proliferated in geometric progression. How, despite the perfection of controlled thermonuclear fusion in 1998, the world continued to burn oil and coal as the skies grew darker and darker. True, the last oil reserves were consumed after the turn of the century, but by then it was too late. The last patch of blue sky was observed off Hawaii in 2008; the atmosphere was permanently contaminated. Worse, the marine life in the world's oceans was killed off by massive garbage dumpings, oil seepage from the world's refineries, certain catastrophic collisions of the giant oil supertankers of the era—accidents that dumped billions of gallons of oil in the already filthy seas. Photoplankton—the marine plants, as you know, that recycled three-quarters of the world's oxygen—was destroyed, thereby drastically reducing the atmosphere's oxygen supply and bringing about a crisis. Our forefathers who had murdered the planet were forced to withdraw into artificially generated environment-cells. The beginning of the Dark Ages had come."

She paused.

"Then the worldwide effort to clean the atmosphere was launched," she continued, surveying her audience, "an effort that unfortunately met with no success. Meanwhile our world supply of artificially produced oxygen continued to deplete itself as we were forced to terminate farm-unit after farm-unit. It was then, twenty years ago, in 2034 that a task force of scientists assembled by President Bennington undertook to realize the last great hope: the conquest of time-travel. By then it was all too apparent that the only hope for the present and the future lay in the past: that our only chance to clean our skies of the pollution was, in a literal sense, to rewrite history, to return to the past century and give our forefathers the secret of clean power—before it was ecologically too late." Again, she paused. "A wild gamble, perhaps," she added quietly, "but one we must all pray will pay off."

She pressed a button on the podium, and the curtains behind the dais silently parted. As Helen watched, two shiny-smooth stainless-steel cylinders appeared, standing side by side at the opposite end of the room. Each cylinder was about thirty feet high and seemed to be approximately fifteen feet in diameter. Neither had any windows; both had, about two feet above the floor, an almost invisible door with a recessed handle. Neither cylinder had any markings painted on it; however, hanging against the wall behind them was an enormous American flag.

There was a low murmur from the audience as it craned its collective neck to see the objects. The Vice-President spoke over the noise.

"Here is the result of twenty years of work and research and over thirty billion Ameri-Dollars expenditure: Time Cylinders Alpha and Beta. This afternoon we will send these two cylinders eight decades into the past, a journey that will require sixteen of our own days. Sixteen days from now, Alpha and Beta will appear side by side on top of the very same mountain this Time Research Laboratory stands upon—except that the year will be 1974. What we now call Time Mountain was then known as Rock Mountain, a hill in a small New England village named Shandy that was abandoned half a century ago because of the pollution. Our two temponauts, Captains Trubee and DeVoe, will take with them cassettes containing the technological data necessary for twentieth-century scientists to understand the construction and operation of thermonuclear-fusion furnaces—twenty-four years before the technology for perpetual clean power was actually discovered. If our temponauts are successful, sixteen days from now our skies should turn blue!"

The audience broke into applause. A pleased smile brightened the previously serious face of the Vice-President. She held up her hands for silence.

"It will, of course, be a dangerous mission," she went on as the hubbub died, "a voyage as perilous and difficult as Columbus' in the fifteenth century or the first landing on the moon in the twentieth. That is why we have decided to send two cylinders; we could not afford to gamble everything—our survival—on one. But speaking for President Bennington—who as you know was unable to attend this ceremony because of"—she hesitated—"the Sickness . . . I can assure you that your government has the utmost faith in the ability and courage of Captain Henry DeVoe of the

United States Navy"—she turned and gestured to a lean man in his thirties behind her who got up from his chair and acknowledged the applause—"and Captain Raymond Trubee. . . ."

To Helen's astonishment, the man with the pig eyes stood up and smiled. *Raymond?* That tall, skinny man with the tiny cruel eyes—could it be that *he* was the god Raymond? Raymond, the self-styled son of Starfire the Creator, who had proclaimed to her and the others he was coming to earth to change the world?

Well, maybe he is, after all, she thought. Except not in a way she had been led to believe.

The audience had risen to applaud the two men, who now joined the Vice-President at the podium, flanking her. She took each by the hand and raised their arms above her head in a political "Victory" sign not unfamiliar to Helen. As the applause again died, the Vice-President lowered her arms and spoke into the microphone.

"Gentlemen, you have trained for this mission for over a year. I know you are eager to begin it, so I won't take up further time with speeches. Time, indeed, is the challenge: for you who are about to journey through it for the first time in history, and for us for whom it is nearly running out. I hardly need repeat that our prayers go with you."

Silence for a moment, after which "The Star-Spangled Banner" blared from hidden loudspeakers. The audience joined the Vice-President in singing a chorus, after which the gray-haired politician planted a maternal kiss on each of the men's cheeks. Then the room again became silent as the temponauts walked off the rear of the dais and approached the two steel cylinders. Helen found herself strangely affected as she watched the bizarre scene. If what she was witnessing was something that would actually take place eighty years in the future in a world that had become almost uninhabitable due to the accumulation of filth, she could certainly understand the thoughts of the people she was watching in this dream-vision. Never to see the sun or the sky, to live one's entire life huddled in artificial environments. . . .

The two men had opened the doors in the cylinders and climbed aboard. Now they stood facing the audience, and waved. There was no response, no shouted "Farewells": only silence. Then they vanished inside the cylinders, closing the doors behind them.

For almost a minute nothing happened. Then the Beta cylinder—the one on the right with Captain DeVoe—became transparent, and vanished. The crowd turned its eyes on the Alpha cylinder, obviously expecting the same astonishing process to take place.

It didn't.

Instead the door opened and Captain Raymond Trubcc reappeared, icy with rage.

"Madame Vice-President," he said, his voice echoing around the large room and bouncing off the plastic dome above which the oily-brown clouds ceaselessly swirled. "There's been a malfunction."

2

"Since when did you start sleeping on the floor?"

She heard the familiar voice only faintly, as through a fog. She opened her eyes and saw Jack standing in front of her. He was holding the silver tray that had been a wedding present from her aunt, and on it was an open bottle of white wine and two glasses. She rubbed her eyes and looked around. She was lying on the floor in the corner of her bedroom where—how long ago? minutes? hours?—she had fainted as the nightmare thing touched her. But the phantom—hallucination?— had vanished and in its place stood her husband holding the tray with the wine.

She slowly got to her feet. She felt slightly nauseous, and a dull headache pounded at the back of her skull.

"Where did you rent the costume?" she said.

"What costume?"

"The Zombie costume."

He looked puzzled.

"What the hell are you talking about?"

She sighed and gave up. "I don't know." She went to the bed and sat down on its edge. "Maybe it *wasn't* you, I really don't care any more." She looked at the wine. "Are we having a party?"

"I thought we might. Isn't it time we declare a truce?"

She smiled. "Why not? I suppose there's no satisfaction in a love-death if there's no love—right? Another of the sayings from Chairman Raymond?"

"What *are* you talking about?"

"I wish you'd stop saying that. You *do* know, but it doesn't matter. Pour me some wine. God knows I need it."

He set the tray on the bed table and filled the glasses, handing one to her. He raised his glass.

"To us," he said.

"Yes, to Romeo and Juliet, the ideal lovers. Or more to the point, Tristan and Isolde."

She drank half the glass, and the wine tasted good, dulling her headache. He sat beside her on the bed.

"This must be what insanity is like," she said. "Not knowing what is real and what is fantasy. Am I insane, Jack?"

"Do *you* think you are?"

"I don't know," she said wearily, then finished the wine and held out her glass for more.

"You're drinking too fast, Helen."

"So what? I want to get gloriously smashed, and then you or Raymond or whoever can reprise your corpse act and finish me off. Won't that be fun?"

He said nothing as he filled her glass. She took another long draft and leaned back on the bed, supporting herself with her elbows. He watched her.

"The amusing thing is," she said, "I don't think you know who he really is, and I do."

"Who?"

"Raymond. You really think he *is* a god, don't you?"

Silence.

"Well, he's not. He's from the future, the awful, hideous future. The great unknown of the next century—except I've seen it. And believe me, the future *doesn't* work. You know, when you think about it, I suppose the greatest nightmare is the future." She sipped some more wine, then said, "You don't believe me, do you? You think I'm ranting on again. But Raymond doesn't want you to know the truth. You wouldn't worship a man from the future, but you'll worship a god." She thought she saw confusion in his eyes: perhaps she had at least planted some seeds of doubt. She sat up and took his hand. "Jack, will you believe me? Will you trust me? Star Child is showing me the *truth* about what's happening to us. Raymond *isn't* a god: he's a madman from eighty years in the future who's twisting your mind to make it a replica of his . . ." She stopped. He wasn't listening to her. A steel door had obviously slammed down over his senses: she could tell it from his cold eyes. He removed his hand from hers and got up from the bed.

"You're upset, Helen," he said softly.

"You're goddam right I'm upset. You've got to listen to me, Jack—you've *got* to—"

He went to the door and looked back.

"Darling, I love you," she said, "and he's going to destroy us unless we learn how to fight him—some way. There *must* be some way, because he's human. He's *not* a god—he's human."

Jack's face was expressionless. He opened the door and quietly went out of the room. She stared at the closed door for a while, then lay back and looked at the ceiling, tears of frustration spilling from her eyes.

"There *must* be some way," she repeated to herself as the drowsiness began to engulf her mind and she once again smelled the faint odor of apple blossoms.

She began to fall asleep.

She found herself standing in front of a large window that was not a window. Rather, she thought, it was some sort of strange monitor, or clock, even. Four feet wide and three feet high, it looked out on a black void against which six vertical beams of pulsating light were projected. The beams were of varying width and color, the far-left beam hot red and string-thin, its pulse shooting upward with great speed. The next beam, to the right, was slightly thicker, slightly slower, and orange. Then yellow, green, pale blue, and finally the farthest beam to the right was white, an inch thick, and seemed to be moving hardly at all.

"That's my tempometer," said a voice she recognized. She turned from the window and saw that she was in a small curved metallic room. Opposite the strange nonwindow was a convex banquette on which Star Child was sitting.

"Where have you been?" she asked quietly.

"I've been having some problems," Star Child said, "which I'll tell you about in a moment. But I wanted you to see the inside of the time cylinder. That window is the tempometer: it measures the time I'm traveling backward through. The six beams of light are seconds, minutes, hours, days, weeks . . . and the thick white beam on the right represents years. I'm going backwards five years a day."

She was watching him, not the tempometer.

"Which of the two are you?" she asked carefully.

As she said it, Star Child slowly vanished and in his place on the banquette appeared the lean, slightly balding man she had seen on the dais in the previous dream. He was wearing his orange tunic.

"I'm Henry DeVoe," he said. "Alias Star Child."

She walked across to the steel floor and stood in front of him, looking into his face. It was as likable a face as his fellow temponaut's was not.

"Why did you pretend to be something you weren't?" she asked. "Why did you pretend to be coming from Tau Ceti?"

"There *was* a point," he said, "but it's rather involved. Why don't you sit down and make yourself comfortable?"

She sat on the white cushion next to him.

"It *is* true, then?" she asked. "The cage dream, and that rather pathetic send-off with the Vice-President?"

"It's true. By the way, I wish it were otherwise, but the fact that a woman finally achieved top political office isn't due to any special enlightenment in our time. The Vice-President happens to be the President's daughter. We don't even hold elections any more—we haven't for forty years. President Bennington was a general who took over the government and made himself President for life. As you heard, he's dying now—finally—from the Pollution Sickness."

"What exactly is that?"

"Our communes, or cells—we had to abandon the cities—are covered by huge domes, like the one you saw, that keep out the pollution. But every once in a while the domes break, or spring leaks. When that happens and a portion of the pollution gets inside, it kills off anyone who breathes it. Three days before we left, the President was walking in his artificial garden. He was standing by the dome looking out at the pollution when the seam cracked. He's probably dead by now."

"The pollution is *that* lethal?" she asked wonderingly.

"It kills in a matter of days."

"But why are you telling me this now?"

"Because when I realized Raymond was invading your mind—which I was afraid he might try to do—I decided I had to tell you the truth, or rather *show* you the truth. I thought-projected into your mind a vision of our world, the world of *your* future. You should be glad you were born when you were, rather than when I was, because, even though your world is certainly far from perfect, it's almost beautiful compared to mine."

"I heard some of it from your Vice-President, but how could everything have gotten so horrible?"

He shrugged. "Democracy didn't work any more, so we became what must seem to you a fascistic society. You know about the pollution, but there was an inner pollution that developed—I suppose you could call it a moral pollution—as lethal in its way as the filth in the air. Morality was already undergoing enormous changes in your time. Violence was becoming a way of life; the traditional sex roles were breaking down; the established religions were losing their force and being replaced by cults and the occult—swamis, gurus, fakirs, prophets. If you can project the trends of your day eighty years into the future, you can get an idea of the morality of my day."

She thought about the love-deaths and Raymond's weird pseudo-philosophy of violence and love.

"Is Raymond typical of the morality of your day?" she asked.

"Very typical. There are some of us who don't approve of the Coupling Rooms and the love-deaths, but we're in the minority, and we don't openly condemn it because we don't condemn *anything*. Most of the Rulers, though, are like Raymond: they enjoy killing. The book your former friend Dr. Akroyd wrote was amazingly perceptive."

"You know the book?" she asked, surprised.

"Oh yes. As does Raymond. In fact, the book is required reading in our universities, and it has had a profound influence on my parents' and grandparents' generations."

"But . . ." She hesitated, her mind numbed by his description of his world. ". . . can anybody kill anyone he wants? It must be murderous chaos. . . ."

"No, only the Rulers can perform love-deaths upon convicted criminals such as the ones you saw in the cage. The Ruled aren't permitted the love-death privilege, though they try to get away with it occasionally and when they're caught they become victims. We also no longer have marriage: we have a system called co-parenthood instead. Birth control is mandatory, and people are allowed no more than two children. But since bisexuality and homosexuality have become pervasive, the majority of the population isn't much interested in raising children anyway. It's the pleasure of sex—the 'kick,' as you might say—that's important. And of course it becomes more and more difficult to keep the kick potent. The love-death is supposed to be the ultimate."

She said, as tactfully as possible, "Have *you* done it?"

He smiled—rather wearily, she thought. It occurred to her that he looked tense.

"No, I'm old-fashioned. I have a co-parent I love, and we have a ten-year-old son named Jerry. But we often ask each other if we should have had Jerry."

"Why?"

"It's an ugly world to bring a child into."

She considered this. "Your Vice-President said thought projection was developed to control the population. Is this what you meant when you told me there was an 'ugly' side to it?"

"Yes. People know that, if they cause political unrest or work against government policies, their dreams will become terror-ridden nightmares. We have a board of psychiatrists and writers who program the dreams and run the devices that generate the electromagnetic fields. Each population cell has one such device, which has an effective range of several miles, enough in any case to reach the limits of the cell. A list of names of potential agitators is given to the board, who transmit the nightmares into the agitators' sleep so that it becomes impossible for them to escape the effect. Many of the dreams deal with such things as walking corpses, attacks of rats or insects. . . . It may sound almost childish, but, as you've experienced, it can be effective."

"Oh, it certainly can. But can thought projection work on the waking mind?" She was thinking of the zombielike creature who had entered her bedroom, as well as the visions of Ben she had seen.

"Yes, but that technique is used only in extreme cases. It can drive the victim insane."

"Then Raymond must be trying to drive me insane."

"He may be," he agreed. "I'm not sure what he's trying to do, but, whatever it is, he doesn't want me to interfere with him."

"How do you know?"

"Because he's murdered me."

"What do you mean?"

"I discovered after I started the time journey that someone had released the oxygen in over half of my tanks. I have less than six hours' supply left."

"And you think Raymond did it?"

"Who else had access to the cylinder?"

"But isn't there anything you can do?"

"Nothing."

"Can't you go back?"

"No. The time-journey is preset. Once you start, you can't change. So . . ." He paused, and she now realized why he seemed so tense. "When this time cylinder arrives in your time-era, I'll be dead. Since my time is running out, let me finish what I have to tell you. You asked why I pretended to be from another world, and the answer involves understanding the danger in going backward in time. You see, to change the past even slightly can alter the future enormously, and no one can predict what the alteration might turn out to be. We wanted to change *one* thing in the past. We wanted to get rid of the pollution in our world by giving you our secret of controlled thermonuclear-fusion power twenty-four years before it was discovered. We decided that if we re-entered the past at the time of the first great energy crisis, when your world first became dramatically aware of the problem of world fuel depletion, your governments would respond quickly to the chance to solve the energy crisis by quick conversion to thermonuclear fusion, which gives off practically no pollution. In that event, the thirty years of polluting that actually occurred from your time until the time the world converted to fusion power would have been eliminated, and our atmosphere would have been saved.

"That was the *one* thing we wanted to change—*had* to change. But the question was, how to do this without changing everything else? If we re-entered the past, allowing the past to *know* we were from the future, the entire history of the next eight decades would be entirely rewritten."

"That might be a good thing, considering how your world has turned out."

"It might. And it might have turned out worse. By avoiding our mistakes, worse mistakes might have been made. We couldn't take that chance. So we decided to re-enter under false pretenses as visitors from outer space, coming into your world to make a one-time visit, then vanishing forever. We knew there was much interest in outer space in your time, so we thought the few people we would need to contact would be inclined to believe us, and the rest of your world wouldn't have to know. That's why I posed as Star Child, and that's why I said I was from Tau Ceti, a star we suspect does in fact have a planetary system with intelligent life. But Raymond has disrupted the whole operation."

"Why?"

He got up from the banquette and walked slowly back and forth in front of her as he talked.

"Raymond Trubee is a strange man," he said, "and a brilliant one in some ways. He is an excellent engineer who solved several of the technical problems involved in building these time cylinders, which is one important reason he was chosen to make the trip. But he's always been interested in religions and the occult, so it's possible he thinks he can set himself up as some sort of god—or devil. He has all the instincts to play the devil." He stopped in front of her and looked into her eyes. "It's going to be *your* job to outwit him—if you're willing to help me."

"What do you want me to do?"

He crossed the room to the time-window and pointed to a red button underneath it.

"Do you see this?"

"Yes."

"This cylinder will materialize on top of Rock Mountain tomorrow at noon. If you're willing to help me, be there and enter the cylinder through the door. Come into this room and push the button." He depressed it, and a small panel in the wall slid silently open. He reached into the recess and pulled out a small metal box. "This contains the cassette. Your husband still has the gun, doesn't he?"

"How did you know?"

"You forget—I'm in your mind. Do you think you can get the gun back?"

"I can try. Why?"

"You may need it. As you saw, the Alpha cylinder had a malfunction, so Raymond's departure was delayed."

"How do you know *that?*" she asked.

"I thought-projected back to the Time Research Lab. I've told them what Raymond has done to me, and they told me about his delayed departure. He didn't leave until six hours after I did. That gives you six hours lead time tomorrow—except Raymond may have told your husband and the others to meet my cylinder and make certain I'm dead, which could mean trouble for you."

"But what am I supposed to *do* with the cassette?"

"Take it to Dr. Jan vanderZee at the Plasma Physics Laboratory at Princeton University—his name and address are in the box. Dr. vanderZee is a Dutch physicist who has won the Nobel Prize and is doing research on thermonuclear fusion. Give him the cassette—he'll know what to do with it."

"Should I tell him where I got it?"

He thought a moment. "Well, it's up to you. Perhaps it's better to tell him nothing, I don't know. The important thing is, once he listens to the cassette, he'll know it came from someone who knows a good deal more than he does."

"But why didn't you just thought-project to him and tell *him* to meet the time cylinders?"

"Our devices can only generate electromagnetic fields for a few miles, and we felt the range would be even less when we were generating through stretches of considerable time as well as space. We had studied the records and knew you lived on the mountain, along with Ben Scovill. Since we couldn't contact vanderZee directly, we decided to use the two of you as our messengers. Raymond was to contact Ben to tell him to cut down the trees for a landing clearing; I was to contact you. Then we would arrive, give both of you the two cassettes . . . a sort of double guarantee, as with the two cylinders . . . and then we'd go back. It didn't work. Raymond contacted Ben but he radically changed the plan—and you know what's happened since. Now I have to depend on you alone. You *must* get this cassette to vanderZee. I don't want to sound overly dramatic about it, but you know enough to understand that the future will literally be in your hands. Will you do it?"

She thought a moment, then nodded.

"It's turning out that you're the last human being I'll talk to in this life," he said, and finally he sounded less tense. "I think I've been very fortunate."

"Thank you." She could think of nothing else to say. . . . What *could* she say?

"No, thank *you*. I've told myself that if Jerry is ever able to come out of the domes and see a blue sky, I'll at least have given my life for something worthwhile." He forced a slight smile, then moved to the edge of the time-window and opened a panel, once again all business. Behind the panel was a vertical row of dials and switches. "I want to return this cylinder to the future, but since I won't be able to activate the controls tomorrow, I'm going to ask you to do it for me. It's simple . . . if you'll come over?" She left the banquette and joined him. He pointed to a digital indicator marked YEAR. "You set this to the year desired, in this case 2054. . . ." He turned a circular dial, and the year numerals flew by until 2054 appeared. "Then the month . . ." Above the year indicator was a similar one that marked the months. He set "November." "And the day . . ." On the uppermost dial he set "27." "The twenty-seventh of November is the day I'm due back. Then you activate this lever"—he pointed to a small red switch—"and you're off. But one thing you must remember: when you come in here tomorrow, fasten the outside door open—you'll see there's a small catch on the side of the cylinder. If you activate the engines with the door closed, you'll go with the cylinder. The outside door has an interlock that breaks the circuit while it's open. Set the dial, activate the switch, then leave the cylinder. The moment you close the door from the outside, the engines will start. Do you understand?"

"I understand."

"I'm writing in the log everything that happened. If you're successful, eighty years from now you'll be something of a national hero."

"That will be something to tell my grandchildren, if I live to have any. Tell me, in your *unchanged* past, what happened to me?"

He shook his head. "I'm not supposed to tell you that."

"Why not? It's going to be different, isn't it? At least somewhat?"

He considered this.

"You won't want to hear it," he finally said.

"I take it I don't live to a ripe old age?"

"I'm afraid you were murdered in 1977."

"By *whom?*"

"Your husband."

"Jack murdered me?"

"He was drunk. According to what we read in the newspaper files he said he got into a fight with you and accidentally fired his gun. He was given ten years for manslaughter. Now you know why we decided to contact you rather than him."

"But then . . . he *hasn't* been changed that much by Raymond, has he?"

DeVoe began to fade from her. "As Dr. Akroyd has said, the potential for violence is in every human mind. Thought projection can only accentuate it." He had almost disappeared. "Good-bye now," he said, his voice distant. "Remember what depends on you."

And he was gone, and she woke up.

3

Now the hall of mirrors was shattered, and she felt relieved: she felt she knew the truth. It was frightening, but not knowing had been worse. She sat up in bed and looked at the clock. Its luminous hands pointed to three-thirty. Time. The universal ocean they all were drowning in, and the future had somehow learned to surface and navigate it. It was awesome. No less was her responsibility. She thought of Jerry DeVoe, the temponaut's son who would not be born for another seventy or so years. Seventy years in the future! She thought back seventy years in the past: 1904. Jerry DeVoe was now to her as she was to a twenty-eight-year-old woman living in the seemingly antediluvian year of 1904—1904, when the pollution generated by the Industrial Revolution was already beginning to foul the earth's air; 1904, the dawn of the automobile age, which would add seventy years of noxious exhaust to the world pollution. And she had now seen the result of eighty more years of pollution. She would never forget those filthy clouds above the plastic dome.

That day, at noon, she would have the power to banish those clouds of the future. It was, indeed, awesome.

Jack. Her once and future executioner, who was to kill her in 1977. She had to get the gun from Jack.

She got out of bed, put on a bathrobe, left the

bedroom and moved quietly across the hall and tried the door to his bedroom. It was unlocked. Carefully, she opened it, listening a moment. The moonlight gave enough illumination so that she could see him on his side in the bed, his naked shoulder a ghostly pale white. She heard his deep even breathing. Slowly she tiptoed into the room and went to the chair he'd hung his pants on. She doubted the gun was in his pants, but she had to be certain. She felt for and found the pockets. Loose change, car keys, half a roll of Lifesavers. In feeling the keys, she clanked them together. The noise was slight but she froze, looking across the room at the bed, listening. The deep breathing continued. She wondered if Raymond was in his mind.

She tried to guess where he would have hidden the gun. There were dozens of places inside the house, hundreds outside. The old hiding place was no good, of course. He wouldn't have been so unimaginative as to hide it there.

The bar. Of course. Jack, the incipient lush (she envisioned that drunken brawl three years in the future when he was to shoot her), would naturally think of the bar. It was probably hidden behind the wine rack.

She went back to the door, trying to tread lightly on the boards she knew squeaked. Reaching the door, she stepped back into the hall, then carefully closed the door.

(Jack opened one eye, watching her leave. He closed it again.)

She agonized her way down the stairs, knowing she couldn't avoid making some noise. The stairs didn't cooperate. Several times she stopped, listening for Jack. Silence.

As she reached the bottom step, the haunting theme of the "Liebestod" slipped into her mind. She tried to force it out but the melody persisted, coiling like smoke through her brain.

She was in the living room now, safe from squeaking boards, on the fieldstone floor. She went to the bar, which was built into the white wooden north wall. Opening the hinged door, she stuck her hand inside the dark opening and felt around the bottles.

The "Liebestod" soared through her brain, now not only the melody but the entire orchestration. She knew it was Raymond. Raymond, toying with her. Raymond providing a soundtrack that would remind her of him. Raymond's signature-tune, the Love-Death. Just as the music became almost deafening, as if someone had turned the hi-fi on full, it stopped.

Silence.

Her hand had explored the entire bar and there was no gun. Irritably, she closed the bar door and looked around the darkened room. Where had he hidden the damned thing?

(Upstairs, Jack lay in the bed staring at the ceiling, idly running his hand over his bare chest. He yawned.)

The chimney? Might he have hidden it there? There was a bricknail above the flue they hung the garage key on when they went away for vacations. Might he have hung the gun on it?

She went to the chimney, opened the flue and reached her hand up. Chimney ash fluttered down on her fingers as she groped. And then she felt the cold steel.

She brought the gun down off the nail.

She went into the dining room, trying to decide where to hide the gun. She went into the dark kitchen. She considered hiding the gun in the freezer compartment of the refrigerator, then rejected the idea. He *might* look in the freezer. Besides, she didn't know that much about guns and it was possible that freezing might jam the damned thing.

The Toyota.

She went out the back door and hurried around the house to the cars. Jack's mustard-colored Volvo station wagon, her gray Toyota. The front window of the Toyota was rolled down, fortunately: she wouldn't have to slam the door. Leaning inside, she put the gun under the front seat, then hurried around the house to the back door and let herself into the kitchen.

She saw the blue-white light shimmering in the air in front of the dining-room door. As she looked at it, it grew larger until it seemed to fill the opposite end of the kitchen. Then in the middle of the aura, which was what it seemed to her, the figure of Raymond began to take shape, apparently floating in the light. He looked as he had in the dreams; an extremely tall, thin man about thirty-five, she judged, with a long face, ski-jump nose and the tiny eyes. His hair, though, was different. In the dreams she remembered it had been an indifferent brown color. Now it was pure white-gold, and she thought irreverently it was either a wig or a botched dye-job. He wore a long white caftan that was richly embroidered around the collar with heavy gold filigree: the effect, she was sure, was intended to be godlike, but it reminded her of a photograph she had once seen of an internationally famous couturier at-home in his chic house in Tangier. Still, if it all was a trick, if the costume was a bit obvious, it was none the less rather effective. She told herself not to be frightened.

She was.

She heard his voice though he didn't move his lips, merely staring at her with those cruel eyes that had seemed to possess an almost hypnotic quality.

"You think you know who I am," the voice said. "You think I am mortal but you are mistaken. I am a god."

"Bullshit."

His face was immobile.

"A god has powers beyond the power of mortal men—"

"Your 'powers' are nothing but some kind of fancy hypnosis or telepathy. And why did you have to kill Captain DeVoe?"

Rather than answering, he raised his long-sleeved arm and pointed at the white refrigerator. The door sprang open, spilling out the light. Inside, coiled, hissing, were huge black snakes crawling over the shelves, and each other. They began slithering out the door.

Helen, who loathed snakes, refused to panic.

"It's an illusion," she said. "I *know* what you're trying to do to me, but you can't frighten me, you can't drive me insane. . . ."

She backed away as the first snake began winding across the floor toward her bare foot.

"You *can't*."

Raymond waved his arm, and the snakes vanished as the refrigerator door slammed shut and the aura floated away from the dining-room door. He now pointed his arm at the darkened doorway. The room beyond glowed with light.

"Behold the truth . . ." said the voice.

"Quit playing the ghost of Christmas past," she snapped.

"Are you afraid to confront the truth?"

"I'm not afraid of *your* truth."

"Then look through the door."

She hesitated; but, convinced the only way to confront him was to face him down, she crossed the kitchen to the door and looked into what had been the dining room. What she saw made her wince and close her eyes.

The room beyond had become Ben Scovill's cellar. Hanging from a ceiling beam was a young man she had never seen but who, she guessed, must be Roger, the hitchhiker. On his forehead was the pentagram brand. His throat was cut, blood had caked down his chest.

Next to him, on the cot, Ben and Jack lay in each other's arms.

She turned to the hovering aura.

"You don't like what you see?" said the voice.

"No." Her voice was low.

"But do you deny it?"

"No, I think it happened."

"Look again."

Reluctantly, she turned back to the dining room. Now the cellar had vanished and was replaced by what appeared to be a motel room—perhaps a room at the River View Motel. It was daylight. On a bed, Jack was making love to Marcia Bernstein.

Helen closed her eyes to the vision. Marcia? That hurt, perhaps more than Ben. Jack with Ben was the new Jack, Raymond's Jack. But Jack and Marcia . . . she suspected that was the old Jack. She turned back to the aura.

"Why are you doing this? To kill my love for Jack?"

"Love me instead. Love *me*."

He opened his arms, as if inviting her into them. She reached to the kitchen counter and picked up a bowl of fruit.

"You go to hell!" she yelled, throwing the bowl with all her strength at the hovering image. The bowl went through the light and crashed against the opposite wall, shattering on the floor.

The kitchen light switched on as the aura vanished.

"What in hell are you doing?" said Jack, standing in the doorway. He had put on his terrycloth bathrobe.

She came up to him and slapped his face. "That's for Marcia Bernstein," she said. Then she spat between his eyes. "And that's for Ben."

She pushed him into the dining room and went through the house to the stairs. For a moment he didn't move.

Then he raised his arm and slowly wiped the spit off his face with the terrycloth sleeve.

Now there was no attempt at all to keep up a façade of normality. She spent the remaining few hours of the night packing her bag in her bedroom; he returned to his room across the hall and locked the door. At dawn, the beginning of the day time would turn inside out and the future would join the present, she walked out of the house, put the suitcase in the rear of the Toyota. As she drove off she wondered if she would ever see her home again.

Her plan: She would drive to town and wait until eleven-thirty. Then she would go back up to the top of the mountain and wait for noon. If the time-cylinder didn't arrive, it meant the entire thing was a mad nightmare. If it did, she would carry out Captain DeVoe's instructions—that is, if "they" didn't stop her. If she succeeded in getting the cassette, she would drive immediately to Princeton, deliver it to Dr. vanderZee and then . . . what?

It promised to be a full day.

It was also a gloomy day: hot, overcast and muggy, mean. She turned on the car radio and got the early-morning news. Thunderstorms were forecast. Wonderful. She switched to another station and the soothing strains of Mozart's Fortieth smiled out from the speaker. Relaxing somewhat, she reached the bottom of the mountain, crossed the Housatonic River and drove down Shandy's main street.

It was quarter to seven. The town was deserted. Parking in front of the Shandy Soda Shoppe, she turned off the engine and leaned back in the seat, listening to the music and waiting for the store to open so that she could order breakfast. Minutes dragged. She turned her head and looked out the window. Past Grayson's Hardware Store across the street, Rock Mountain rose in the distance, the gray clouds crowning its peak obscuring the sun's light, if not its heat. Clouds. Pollution. The death of a planet.

And the death of morality. She believed what DeVoe had told her of the future, because the seeds of the future's corruption were already planted in her own time. Could she doubt the death of democracy after the chancre of Watergate? Wasn't the power of the government already overwhelming? And it took little imagination to see the embryo of the love-death "privilege" in the rising sea of violence in the Sixties and Seventies of her own century. That Norton's book had become required reading in the universities of the future was a rich irony, considering the fact that the future had returned to transform him into a living example of his own thesis; but his book was not to blame for the future. Though she hadn't believed its lurid thesis at first, now she had to admit it probably had captured an insidious trend of the times, a trend that the changing morality of the twentieth century would only accelerate, culminating in the Coupling Rooms of Raymond's day. How sad it was, she thought. The love-death concept was really the death of love, and no wonder the DeVoes had debated the wisdom of bringing a child into that loveless world of the next century. She wasn't sure which pollution was the more terrifying: the pollution of the planet's atmosphere, or the inner pollution of the planet's soul. She wondered if, in some way, the one had caused the other.

She looked at her watch. Five to seven. She had awakened from the dream at three-thirty that morning, and so Captain DeVoe's six hours would soon be up; for him, at least, the nightmare of the future would be over. She envisioned him lying on the metal floor of that strange room in front of the strange tempometer gasping for breath as the last of the oxygen was used. . . . Where was he? Again, she looked at the top of the mountain. He was there already, except he wasn't. There geographically, but somewhere else in the ocean of time. . . .

She turned and saw Art Siebert, the owner of the Soda Shoppe, come out of his small brown clapboard house next to the store and head for the shop to open it. Art was the father of the first victim, Judy Siebert, and she wondered if she should tell him what had happened to his daughter. She decided against it.

There would be time for that later, time to tell everything. Now no one would believe her. Now there was one thing of importance: to get the cassette to the professor in Princeton. She got out of her car and walked to the store.

"Good morning," she said.

Art, who was in his sixties, was normally taciturn; the disappearance of his daughter had made him especially dour. Now, however, he nodded and managed a half-smile.

"Morning, Mrs. Bradford. What are you doing in town this early?"

"I'm going to Boston," she said, deciding it was better not to let him know. Art might be one of them, after all.

He unlocked the door, and she followed him inside. The Soda Shoppe was itself a decorational time warp, a period piece out of the mid-Thirties. The long marble soda counter with the wireback stools; the fading Coca-Cola signs above the mirror juxtaposed with Dr. Pepper and Pepsi signs; the rows of half-clean glasses; the pervasive odor of old grease. Opposite the counter, the four dark-wood booths. She went to the nearest booth and eased herself in on the hard wooden seat. Art puttered around the shop, turning on the coffee, unlocking the cash register. Hot. Humid. A wretched start to a crucial day.

"What would you like, Mrs. Bradford?" said Art, appearing beside her.

"I think just coffee and toast, please."

"Jam or honey?"

"Honey."

He went back to the counter to put the toast on. A wasp buzzed around the plate-glass window and finally settled on an aging window display of Johnson & Johnson trusses (which Art hadn't sold in ten years).

A state-police car pulled up behind her Toyota and two troopers got out. She recognized them. One, the tall redhead, was Sergeant Bixby, the man she had confessed Ben's murder to. The other, young trooper was Rydell. As they entered the shop, she instinctively tensed, hoping they wouldn't see her. But why was she afraid? If they wouldn't believe her, it wasn't her fault. . . . Bixby spotted her, and she nodded slightly. He nodded in return, then seated himself at the counter and ordered a cup of coffee. Rydell sat next to him and ordered tea.

She briefly wondered why he hadn't spoken to her, but then she decided he was too embarrassed to say anything after yesterday. Poor man, what could he say to mad Mrs. Bradford? "Good morning, ma'am, any new murders today?" "The Great God Raymond show up yet?" "Has the world entered the New Age of the new religion of love-death?"

She didn't blame him for not speaking.

She watched his brawny blue back and the thinner back of Rydell next to him. Art had already served them their coffee, which was rather annoying since they had just arrived. She supposed Art had to be especially nice to the troopers. There weren't any police in Shandy, after all. The troopers were it, so far as law-and-order was concerned.

Art brought her the plate of toast (burned), the pat of butter (old), and the cup of coffee (which smelled rancid). Then he returned to the counter. She poured sugar and cream into the coffee in a vain attempt to disguise its acrid taste.

It was then Norton Akroyd came in the shop.

Norton, prophet of the future, Norton the enemy. Again, she tensed. He walked past the two troopers, looked at her, nodded slightly, then pulled out one of the wire-backed stools and sat down at the counter. This made no sense. Norton was single, but he was fastidious about his food and she couldn't believe he would ever eat breakfast in this gastronomic disaster area. Besides, the troopers had talked to him yesterday; certainly they would say something about it now, even if they were too embarrassed to talk to her. And yet, no one was saying a word.

She found her hand was shaking as she picked up her coffee cup. She stirred her coffee, watching Norton's back. Norton, such a short time ago one of her closest friends, now one of "them.". . . .

She knew she was thinking wildly, and for the hundredth time wondered if she were not indeed mad. It was certainly possible. The dreams could all be dreams, the illusions, illusions. . . . Even Ben, she supposed, *might* have been an illusion. Or, rather, she might have *thought* he said what he said before she shot him, if in fact, she did shoot him. What if Norton hadn't reloaded the gun . . . ? What if Ben had said something as innocuous as "What are you doing in my cellar, Mrs. Bradford?" and she *thought* he was talking about Raymond the new god and she shot him—why? Because she hated him? Because she thought her husband had become his lover? It was possible. . . . And Marcia Bernstein. She had always wondered about Jack and Marcia. Had Raymond showed her the truth about them, or was it her overworked imagination trying to confirm her long-time suspicions? Had there been worms in the subsoil of her complacent former life in Shandy, snakes of lust in the icebox all along? How clever of her to select such metaphors . . . if they were. . . .

Jeremy Bernstein walked into the shop. As with Norton and the sergeant, Jeremy nodded to her, said nothing, sat down at the counter.

They were, she decided, her guards. They knew she was going to the mountain to meet the time-cylinder, and they were going with her. To do what? Kill her? Possibly. She only knew they were in the shop to watch her. Were the state troopers in on it too? Was that possible? But why not? If Raymond could take over one mind, he could take over others, and wasn't it smart to have the troopers on your side? Of course.

She had to get out. She fished a dollar bill from her purse and left it on the table, then got out of the booth and started toward the door. Art Siebert watched her from the grill where he was heating an English muffin. His customers didn't turn around. Odd. The watchers weren't watching. Nor were they trying to stop her.

She opened the door and walked out onto the sidewalk. She turned and looked back through the window. *Now* they were watching: heads were turned, eyes were staring at her. Trying to smother panic, she hurried to the car. But where could she go? As she started the engine, she thought of Ben's house. Perfect. Ben was dead, and even Raymond couldn't raise the dead, except in dreams. The bodies had been moved out of the "chapel"; the place was safe, unconsecrated. Most important, it was near the mountaintop. She would go there and wait. She started the car and managed a U-turn, half-hoping the troopers would run out and give her a ticket. At least that would be normal, real.

No one came out.

She drove back through town, recrossed the Housatonic and started up Rock Mountain Road. She wouldn't have been surprised to see their cars in the mirror, following her. Or perhaps a roadblock, stopping her. Nothing would have surprised her at this point.

No one followed her. No one stopped her.

She passed the driveway to her house and slowed down to look in. Jack's Volvo was still parked in front of the garage. Everything appeared normal. (Could it be possible that everything *was?*)

She continued up the road over the top of the hill, then down the north face toward Ben's farm. Pulling into his driveway, she drove up to the house and parked. She looked around. The place was deserted, the house sagging, the red barn empty, the fields cleared of cattle and equipment. Dead.

She looked at her watch. Twenty-five to eight. Over

four hours to wait. She'd sit in the car. That way, if someone came she could quickly escape down the road. She turned on the radio and tried to relax. Mozart had been replaced by Strauss. *The Artist's Life*. Dum dee dum dee dum dee dum. The lilting waltz theme filled the car with sunshine.

Outside, the sky was growing darker.

4

The storm broke at ten-twenty.

The sky had grown almost black, the humidity stifling. Distant rumblings of thunder from the west had grown louder as she watched the lightning jab from the sky. Finally the stillness was broken by a gust of wind, and the first fat raindrops began splatting on the car roof. She knew the safest place in a thunderstorm was an enclosed car, but in her present frame of mind the prospect of sitting out a storm in her tiny Toyota was hardly a pleasant one. Besides, after two hours, her legs were cramped.

She decided to see if she could get into the house. Putting the gun and the bullets into her purse, she got out of the car and ran through the rain to the back of the house to try the rear window. Again, it was unlocked. Shoving it open, she crawled into the kitchen just as the rain began to come down in earnest. She closed the window and brushed herself off as she looked around. The kitchen was still a mess, just as it had been the day before when she had broken in and, later, shot Ben. . . . Her eyes went to the trapdoor in the corner. Closed. Ben, Ben, that beautiful thing of evil she had killed . . .

Shuddering at the memory, she went into the living room and looked around. Again, unchanged, although there was *something* different . . . The smell. Yes, of course. There was a faintly sweet smell she hadn't remembered. . . .

She went to one of the ancient Colonial windows and looked out through the unclear glass and plastic. She couldn't see too well, but she didn't need to. The full fury of the storm had broken now, and the wind, the lightning and the thunder competed for supremacy. She was glad she'd come into the house.

Again, she became conscious of the sweet smell, and this time she recognized it. Incense. She remembered the altar in the basement. But the chapel had been unconsecrated, the house was deserted.

Wasn't it?

She turned around from the window, half expecting to see—what? There was nothing. Just the smell, perhaps stronger now. And, outside, the beating rain, the crashing thunder . . .

Cautiously, she returned to the kitchen and went to the trapdoor. Grabbing the handle, she tugged it open. The incense smell rushed out at her. Leaning the door against the wall, she took a few steps down, her hand on the light switch. She didn't need to turn it on: someone had lighted candles. Not only on the altar, where the incense smoked, but all around the room burned dozens of candles, filling the ancient cellar with their glow and lighting the bodies resting on their white-draped catafalques.

Ben. He was there in his pine coffin, directly in front of the altar, as though in the place of honor. Ben, looking asleep, his eyes closed, his profile outlined by the candlelight, his body dressed in a clean white robe, his hands folded over his stomach. Flanking him were Judy Siebert and Betty Fredericks, each in a pine coffin, each dressed in a white robe similar to Ben's, each clasping in her folded hands a red rose. Betty Fredericks' head had been repositioned at her neck. A white scarf modestly concealed the separation.

Along the north wall was Roger, the hitchhiker, in his coffin. He, too, was in a white robe, but they'd been less modest with him. Not only was the pentagram brand still on his forehead, but the red-brown scar of his gutted throat was plainly visible. There was a fifth body. She came up to the coffin next to Roger's and looked at the face of Doug, the truck driver. Who is he? Who had killed him? Who had arranged all the bodies so neatly in this shrine?

For that's what it apparently was. The candles, the bodies, the incense. A shrine to Raymond. Like the catacombs of ancient Rome where the early Christian martyrs were laid out and venerated, here the first Raymond martyrs had been put on display. Ghouls, she thought. Jack, Jeremy, Norton . . . she envisioned them buying the coffins from some puzzled undertaker, transporting the bodies, dressing them in the white robes . . .

She shuddered, nauseated by the mechanics of death. She wanted to be away from this sweet-smelling sepulcher, this house of the dead. Taking a last look at Ben's face, she returned to the stairs and went back up to the kitchen, closing the trapdoor on the shrine.

The worst of the storm had passed now. The sky was becoming lighter. She looked out the window she had climbed through. Above her the rocky land stretched to the top of the mountain, the trees bending and swaying in the wind, the rain whipping across the fields. The top of the mountain was waiting.

She glanced at her watch: 10:45.

In one hour, she told herself, she would start to walk up the hill.

She thought of the eerie shrine beneath her and decided—even though the car was cramped—she would spend the next hour in the Toyota.

It was cool now, the coolness of after-the-storm. The sky was clearing, and the west was radiant with yellow and lobster-meat-pink clouds against the lovely blue sky. Raindrops sparkled on the field grass and clover as she made her way up the hill, her right hand ready to take out the Smith & Wesson from her shoulderbag. So far she had seen no one. Neither at the house nor on the hill. She wondered if it were possible none of them would appear. She told herself that was unlikely. Surely Raymond would have sent one of them to check on DeVoe. Except why had Raymond killed him? That still made no sense to her.

She had left the Toyota at 11:45, and it took her ten minutes to reach the landing on the mountain top. As she caught her breath, she looked around her at the spectacular view. The sky, half-unclouded now, its new-washed air sparkling, was so clear she judged she could see ten miles. How beautiful the land was; how sad that DeVoe would never see it.

(That is, if Captain DeVoe had been real and the time-cylinder actually showed up. If it didn't, then what in the world was the answer to the shrine and the love-deaths? Norton. . . . She'd considered that, early on, but now she was convinced she'd seen the future. . . .)

She walked to the row of pines that had been left standing at the south edge of the clearing, the row she thought was to serve as a screen to hide the time-cylinders from the town below. She looked down at her house. Jack's Volvo was gone. She wondered if he had come up here. . . . She looked around the clearing. No one.

It occurred to her that it was more than passing odd that she had seen no one since that morning at the Soda Shoppe. Where *were* they all? What had happened to her guards?

Noon.

She turned her eyes from her watch to the clearing. Nothing.

Did this mean she was mad after all, that the whole business—the dreams, the deaths—all was the creation of imagination? Or of Norton's powers?

And then she saw it—*magically*, form began to emerge from void, as she'd imagined the creation of the stars and planets, the formation of hydrogen atoms out of the emptiness of outer space. As she watched, awe-struck, the outlines of the cylinder silently appeared, the same vertical steel cylinder she had seen in the dream with DeVoe. Here, truly, dream was becoming reality. Relief . . . she was *not* mad, her sanity was surely vindicated. The miracle was happening, the time-cylinder from the future was materializing in the present; time indeed had been breached.

The proof.

She waited for nearly a full minute after it had materialized, looking at the strangely beautiful object, half-expecting someone else to step from the surrounding trees into the clearing. No one did; all was silent. She started walking toward the cylinder.

When she reached the door, she put out her hand and gingerly touched it as a final test of its reality. The steel felt cold and smooth. She depressed the latch and the door opened. A slight "whoosh" of sound as fresh air rushed in and the exhausted atmosphere of the inside rushed out. Air. The journey had been made for air. Lack of it had killed DeVoe.

Remembering his instructions, she carefully locked the door open by latching it to the side of the cylinder. She stepped inside. A tiny compartment, bare except for a short ladder leading up. She began climbing the half-dozen feet to the compartment above. As her face came over the floor level, a hand bumped her forehead. She drew back: it was Captain DeVoe's hand. He had died reaching out for the ladder, perhaps in some final attempt to escape the inevitable.

She cleared the ladder and stepped into the room she had already seen. She looked down at the body. A man born long after she had died was now dead before he was born—and she was looking at his corpse. She briefly wondered if perhaps she should try to take him out of the cylinder and bury him, but decided against it. He belonged to the future. His body should be returned home.

She went to the time-window. The pulsating lights had stopped now, and the window was black. She reached under it and pressed the red button. The panel slid open. Reaching in, she took out the small metal box and looked at it.

The power of the sun. She held its secret. Oddly, all she could think of was that it seemed incredibly small to hold such an immense secret. She put the box in her purse, next to the gun.

She went to the panel next to the time-window, opened it and looked at the dial indicators. They were set for November 27, 2054. All she needed to do was throw the red switch. . . . Had she locked the door open? The thought of accidentally sending herself into the hideous world of the future was not a pleasant one. No, she had latched the door open. She was safe.

She pushed the switch. Silence. What had she expected? The roar of strange engines powerful enough to send the cylinder outside of time? She didn't know, but somehow the silence was odder than any noise could possibly be.

She walked across the room to the ladder, pausing beside Captain DeVoe for a final look. There must be something she could do, some small tribute. . . . She looked in her purse, scrounged around between the metal box and the gun until she found a scrap of paper and ballpoint pen. Taking out the paper, she looked at it. An old grocery bill. A marvelous tribute to a national hero. Still, it was better than nothing. Using the wall, she wrote the following note on the back of the bill:

To Jerry DeVoe—
   Your father was a fine man. Be proud of him.
                    [Signed] Helen Bradford,
                            August 1974

She found a safety pin in her purse and pinned the note on the dead man's back. It wasn't much, she reflected, but she felt better for doing it.

She took a last look at the strange room, then climbed back down the ladder and stepped out of the cylinder. She looked about. The clearing was still empty. Maybe they didn't give a damn. She turned back to the cylinder, unlatched the door.

She slammed it shut.

She stepped back, as if unconsciously afraid of being sucked into the wake as the cylinder started its return journey. It began to agitate, as if, perhaps, the molecules of the complex machine were rearranging themselves outside of time. It became more and more transparent, like a ghost ship.

And then it was gone, as silently, and magically, as it had arrived.

She walked across the clearing to the trees, then started down the mountain toward her Toyota.

PART V

The
Ascension

1

Norton Akroyd had just finished showering and shaving and was half-dressed when he heard the buzzer of his front door.

"Just a minute!" he called. It was ten minutes before five and he had an important engagement at six—the most important of his life. He wasn't pleased to be interrupted now. He slipped on his Gucci loafers (Norton liked expensive clothes, and tonight especially he wanted to look his best) and buttoned his white shirt. Then he hurried out of his bedroom, just as the buzzer rang again.

"Coming!" He made his way past his desk, strewn with photographs of an assortment of murder victims. He had been working on his new book, the research of which had taken on such a dramatic new dimension lately. Murder. The phenomenon he'd studied so dispassionately. He wasn't dispassionate anymore. And the Master . . . what incredible satisfaction when the Master had told him that he knew his first book well and admired it extravagantly. He didn't understand *how* the Master knew it, except that, of course, a supreme being knew everything.

As much as he feared, loved and venerated the Master—and Norton's emotional response to the incredible dreams was a mixture of all three—at the same time he rather envied him too. Was it right to envy god? He couldn't help it. He envied his power and his knowledge. Why shouldn't he? For all his years of studying the mind, he knew so little. During the hundreds of analyses he had conducted in his professional career, the best he could do was peek into the recesses of his patients' minds, while the Master *entered* his own mind. How incredible. (And how ironic, in retrospect, was Jack Bradford's notion that he, Norton, had been hypnotizing Jack and Helen. As if he could do what the Master could do, as if he had the Master's power . . .) Perhaps the Master would share some of his power with his apostles. Hadn't the army of Christian saints performed miracles attested to by witnesses and challenged by Devil's advocates? Why shouldn't Raymond's saints be able to do the same? . . . (And yet at times Norton suspected that perhaps Jack had been right after all, that perhaps Raymond *was* a projection of his, Norton's, ego, and that in some way—Norton had no idea how, at least no longer, if he ever once did—he had been able—unconsciously?—to exercise his influence on the minds of his friends. It *was* strangely coincidental that Raymond knew his book, that so many of his ideas were being acted out in reality and his special areas of interest were being tapped by these presumably outside forces. It was the characters of *his* friends that were being turned inside out. *They* were performing these love-deaths. Was it possible that he, Norton, was the god Raymond and didn't even know it? The idea was dizzying, dismaying, yet it explained so many things, explained how Raymond could enter *his* mind. He remembered how—before he had started having the dreams—he had told a frightened and confused Helen that Star Child and Raymond were projections of a benign and malignant side of her subconscious. But perhaps it was *his* subconscious. Nor did he believe himself a victim of schizophrenia. If Raymond did indeed come from his brain, then *he* had the godlike power to project his thoughts to others, coercing them to submit their wills to his. . . . Was, in fact, Raymond the embodiment of the lust and violence he'd always sensed within himself but had struggled so long to suppress in favor of a better, more acceptable self—Star Child? . . .)

. . . He had to dismiss such notions as dangerous, altogether too terrifying in the responsibility they conferred. Raymond was the new divinity and he, Norton, was not god but only an adoring apostle. . . . (And yet, the memory of the idea lingered on seductively.)

As a disciple, though, he had yet to perform a love-death, and he knew that until he did he would never be admitted into the Master's total confidence. The others had: Ben, Jack, Jeremy. Only he had yet to prove his devotion to the Master, and the Master would want to know why (but what if the Master were himself?). Self-punishment? Was it because he didn't have the nerve?

The buzzer rang a third time, and Norton angrily opened the door.

"Yes?"

Outside stood Lyman Henderson. The obese headmaster looked troubled. "Norton, I'm sorry to barge in on you like this, but I'm terribly worried about Helen Bradford. Can I see you for a minute?"

Of all times for this fat idiot to hold me up. . . . Doesn't he know that in an hour the most important event of . . . doesn't he *know?* Of course he doesn't, but still . . .

"Come in," he said sullenly.

He held the door as Lyman lumbered into the living room.

"Sorry the place is such a mess," said Norton, closing the door. "I've been working on my new book."

Lyman was staring at the glossies of murder victims.

"Norton, how do you stand these pictures? Don't they turn your stomach?"

Norton hurriedly gathered the photos together, wishing he'd filed them away earlier.

"One gets used to it."

"Used to *that?*"

"Do you think doctors stop operating because they don't enjoy looking at intestines?" snapped Norton, his irritation growing. "When your subject is murder, you have to accept the fact that it's bloody."

Lyman was staring at him, obviously surprised at normally mild-mannered Norton's sharpness.

"I suppose you're right. . . ." he said.

"Of course I'm right."

He stuffed the photos in the top drawer of the file cabinet and slammed the drawer shut. He had to get rid of Lyman! He *couldn't* be late. . . .

"Now, what about Helen?" he said, turning back to his employer.

"Do you think it would be stretching the laws of hospitality to offer me a chair?" The headmaster was getting as testy as Norton. The psychiatrist backed down.

"I'm sorry. Please, sit down. Here, on the sofa. . . ."

Lyman eased into the sofa like the *Hindenburg* nuzzling its mooring mast.

"Norton, you said yesterday that Helen is very sick. Of course, all of this came as a complete surprise to me. I knew Jack was drinking, but I had no idea things had gotten as bad as apparently they are. . . . How long have you been treating Helen?"

"Only a short while."

"And what are these dreams you mentioned?"

Norton shrugged. "Nothing so unusual. Creatures from outer space, nightmares . . ."

"And you don't find that unusual?" asked Lyman, amazed.

"Not especially. They're what psychiatrists encounter every day. Of course, there's the possibility that her mind has been irreversibly affected, but it's too soon to be certain."

"Well, I don't like it, Norton. I don't like it at all. Those manic accusations, saying Jack is a murderer . . . if she took to saying that in front of the students it would be terrible for the school's public image. The problem is we'll be opening in ten days, and, fond as I am of Helen, I'm wondering if I shouldn't hire a replacement for her?"

Norton was only half-listening. His attention was focused on the letter opener on his desk.

"Norton, I wish you'd pay attention."

"Hm? Oh . . . sorry. Yes, I see your point, and perhaps you're right. Perhaps you'd better get someone to substitute for Helen. I can't guarantee she'll be better by the opening. She may even get worse. . . ."

Lyman leaned forward and lowered his voice, a worried look on his round face. "There's no chance she's telling the truth, is there? I mean, about Jack. After all, he's been behaving as strangely as Helen. . . . That outburst the other morning on the tennis court—what the hell was he talking about, saying you had 'zapped his mind'?"

"I told you they both seem to have paranoid persecution fantasies."

"What if they're not fantasies? There's a number of people missing around here. Not only Judy Siebert, but that woman in Fairfax. And I heard on the radio this morning that a truck driver over in Wingdale has disappeared. People are getting nervous. . . ."

Norton said softly, "How many times have I told you we're all potential murderers?"

But are you, Norton Akroyd? Can *you* do it? You, of all people, should . . .

Lyman Henderson was staring at the head of the psychology department, who was certainly acting strangely. He felt uncomfortably nervous. "If that possibility exists," he said, "even the *remote* possibility, then there's no question that I'll have to get them both off the campus. Do you think I should tell the police?"

"The police?" laughed Norton. "The police are killers, too."

What in Christ's name is going on? thought Lyman. Why is the man trembling so? What's he holding behind his back?

He rose from the sofa.

"Norton, is something the matter?"

"I think you'd better leave," Norton said, his voice hoarse.

"Are you all right?"

"Get out," he yelled. "Just get *out!*" Before *I* kill you, he thought. Before I do it. Get out before I do it, because I *want* to do it. I want to . . .

Lyman Henderson was backing to the door, his face white.

"Jesus Christ, you're as sick as they are!" he muttered as he groped for the doorknob. Finding it, he opened the door and quickly backed his bulky body through, slamming the door behind him. The moment it was closed, Norton ran across the room and plunged the letter opener into the wood.

"I couldn't do it, Master . . . I *couldn't*. I failed you . . ."

He slid down the door and sank in a heap on the floor. He had ruined everything. How could he face the Master now? How *could* he? Now the Master would know he had been weak. The Master hated weakness. I can't face him. . . .

He got to his feet and stumbled into his bedroom.

Taking a suitcase from his closet, he began stuffing his clothes into it.

Helen didn't reach Princeton until almost six o'clock in the evening, at which time she was so hungry she decided the fate of the future could wait long enough for her at least to get some dinner. She went to the Nassau Tavern and ate a solid meal. Then, after asking directions to Hodge Road, where Dr. vanderZee's house was located (it was too late for him to be at the laboratory), she got back into her car and drove down the main street of the town past the charming pseudo-Gothic eating halls with their splendid, shadowed towers toward the heavily carved monument to George Washington. The evening was pleasantly cool after the meteorological fireworks of the morning, and the town was lovely with its tree-lined streets and handsome houses. Hodge Road was particularly lovely, the houses particularly handsome . . . she thought Dr. vanderZee's Nobel Prize money must come in handy to help his mortgage payments in this obviously expensive area. His house was not as big as his neighbors', but it was hardly small. It was surrounded by a quarter acre of well-tended lawn, and the planting was lush. No one was outside, despite the beauty of the evening; a Buick station wagon, however, was parked in the driveway.

She went to the front door and rang the bell. After a while a gray-haired woman in a light-blue dress opened the door.

"Yes?" She reminded Helen of an English country type out of an Agatha Christie novel.

"I want to see Dr. vanderZee," she began. "I know this is unusual but it's an emergency."

The woman looked her over. "My husband just started dinner——"

"Please—it really *is* important."

Mrs. vanderZee stepped back and held the door. She didn't appear too happy.

"Come in, please."

Helen stepped into a small tiled foyer, then was led through the modern living room into a sterile dining room where a thin man in his fifties was sitting at a glass-topped table. He stood up as Helen entered the room. He had white hair, not unpleasant features, and was dressed casually. He looked at her through square pilot glasses that were a generation too young for him.

"Dr. vanderZee? My name is Helen Bradford."

The physicist looked inquiringly at his wife, who shrugged.

"I've come from Connecticut," continued Helen, reaching into her purse, "to bring you this." She pulled out the metal box and handed it to the scientist, who opened it.

"What is it?" he asked, pulling out the cassette. He had a Dutch accent; his wife's was English.

"I suggest you listen to it. That will be easier than my trying to explain. I think you'll see that it's very important."

He looked confused. "I have a machine in my study. . . ." he said, uncertainly. "I suppose . . ." He seemed to make up his mind. "Well, all right. You wait here. I'll be back in a few minutes."

He left the room and his wife took her seat at the table.

"Would you care for something?" she said.

"No, thank you. I've just eaten."

"A glass of wine then?"

"Well, that might be nice."

"Please sit down."

She pulled out the side chair and sat down as Mrs. vanderZee filled a glass from the decanter. She passed the wine to Helen, saying, "Now, my dear, what is this all about?"

Helen sipped the cool Chablis.

"I'd rather let the cassette speak for itself."

"You come all the way from Connecticut to deliver a tape you refuse to discuss to a man you've never met? That seems rather extraordinary."

Helen said nothing, silently agreeing that it *was* extraordinary, but she hardly needed Mrs. vanderZee to remind her of that. Several minutes passed in somewhat hostile silence; Mrs. vanderZee was making it plain she didn't appreciate having her dinners interrupted by strangers. Finally her husband returned. He didn't have the look of stunned awe that Helen had assumed after listening to what must represent to a scientist a sort of epiphany. Rather, he looked annoyed.

"Young lady, is this some sort of joke?" he said, coming to the table, on which he now placed the cassette.

"What do you mean?"

"There's *nothing* on that tape."

She blinked.

"Now I'm afraid I must ask you to leave."

"It's Raymond," she said. "He must have erased the tape before DeVoe even started."

"Raymond?"

The doorbell rang.

"It seems we're to starve this evening," grumbled Mrs. vanderZee, getting up from the table. As she went into the living room, her husband came over beside Helen.

"*Was* there something on that tape?" he said.

"Yes. And it was important."

"What was it?"

"The secret of the technology of controlled thermonuclear fusion."

"Then you *are* joking. No one knows that."

"The future does."

"I'm sure of that, but it's not much help. . . ."

"The cassette was a gift from the future. Or at least it was intended to be. The idea was to give us clean power twenty-four years before it actually was developed, and over thirty years before the world converts to it. That way the earth's atmosphere eighty years from now would be cleaned of the pollution. And I don't blame you if you think I'm crazy. But you would have believed me if you'd heard what was on the tape."

"Jan . . . ?" said Mrs. vanderZee from the living-room doorway. They turned to see her standing in front of Sergeant Bixby and Trooper Rydell. Dr. vanderZee looked at them with growing alarm.

"My name's Bixby," said the redhead in a pleasant tone. "We've come to escort you and your wife and Mrs. Bradford back to Connecticut."

"Connecticut?" said the physicist. "Don't be ridiculous; I have no reason to go to Connecticut—"

"We realize this is something of an imposition, Dr. vanderZee, but . . ." He placed his hand suggestively on his holster. Helen stood up and said softly, "Do what they say, doctor."

"Would someone explain . . . ?"

"Everything will be explained in Shandy," interrupted Bixby, his voice somewhat less pleasant. "We have two cars outside. And we have a driver to take your car back, Mrs. Bradford. I'd appreciate your moving quickly as possible."

Helen came up to him. "I see you've changed your mind about my story," she said.

"Your husband wants the gun back," was all that he said. He held out his hand. Helen hesitated, then took the Smith & Wesson from her purse and gave it to him.

Dr. vanderZee said, "Is there any reason for my wife to go?"

Sergeant Bixby nodded. "There is."

Husband and wife exchanged worried, confused looks. Then they and Helen and the two troopers started toward the front door.

Jack Bradford had gambled on a dream, and now that it was about to become reality his mind was being stretched by a dozen conflicting emotions. He told himself that Raymond had to be what he claimed rather than what Helen said he was, that there was no other possible explanation for the miracles that had been performed in his mind. But Jack had committed *murder*. What if Raymond indeed were from the future, as Helen said? What if he were only human, what if the beginning of the New Era was a hoax, what if Raymond couldn't protect him and the others, what if they weren't above the law? But that couldn't be. Bixby and the two other troopers were on their side. Or at least seemed to be. . . . Everything *seemed*. What really *was?*

Who was Star Child, the false god? Raymond claimed he had destroyed him, but still . . . who *was* he? What if he weren't false? What if the religion of love-death was nothing but homicidal mania? Yet what Raymond had whispered to him in the dreams had the biting edge of perception. Wasn't in fact the story of the world one of bloodshed, of war and rape? Why, as Raymond asked, hadn't other religions ever really taken hold? Could anyone seriously talk of the triumph of Christian good in a world dominated by evil and misery? Or when confronted with the dumbfounding statistic of the hundreds of millions killed in the name of Christianity and other religions?

So Raymond might have perceived the truth. Jack had to admit the crimes he'd committed in Raymond's name had been nearly as intoxicating as predicted. At the same time there was a reservoir of guilt in Jack's mind along with his fear of having to pay the price for what he'd done if this mysterious force that had so swiftly dominated his life proved to be less than all-powerful.

That evening, when he joined Marcia and Jeremy Bernstein at the summit of Rock Mountain to await the arrival of the self-proclaimed god, Jack's mood was anything but placid. He braced himself against the strong wind that was blowing and stared at the center of the clearing, wondering what would happen to his life now and whether the whole experience had been some kind of bizarre, sustained dream.

It was then he realized Norton was not there.

"Where's Norton?" he asked the Bernsteins. Jeremy, whose bearded face looked glazed, shrugged and said he didn't know.

"But he wouldn't miss *this,*" Jack said, and then a new thought struck him—or, rather, an old one returned with new force, offering the alternative explanation.

"What if," he said hesitantly, "I was right about Norton?"

The Bernsteins looked at him.

"What do you mean?"

"What if none of this has actually happened? What if Norton's only made us *believe* it's happened . . . by hypnotizing us?"

"Oh come on," Marcia said. "Where would he learn to do that? On a trip to Tibet?"

"I don't know and I don't know how he did it . . . if he did . . . but isn't that at least a possibility? He's a psychiatrist, he's studied and no doubt used hypnosis. . . ."

"Jack," Jeremy said gently, "you're trying to deny the beauty of what's happening to us, the beauty of Raymond."

"Do you think what he's done to us is beautiful?"

"The confirmation that there is something beyond, something greater than us . . . that's what I've wanted to believe all my life. *That's* beautiful."

The wind gusted with new force as Jack looked at the others. "Then where is Norton?" he said.

Jeremy now pointed to the center of the clearing. "Is *that* illusion?" he said, and the others turned to look. A time-cylinder was taking substance. The three of them stood transfixed as the steel cylinder silently took shape. When it had materialized, there was a wait of almost a minute before the door slowly opened. The tall man with the white-gold hair and the white filigreed robe appeared. He looked around him; then he stepped out of the cylinder and turned hs eyes upward to the sky. The expression on his face became wondrous, like that on the faces of his apostles, as he stared at the rich blue of the evening sky, the setting sun a glory of gold as it dipped toward the mountain tops to the west. For nearly half a minute he stood staring upward, the wind blowing his hair and his robe. Then he lowered his gaze to the apostles, smiled and opened his arms wide.

"Beloved brethren," he said, "I bring you tidings of great joy: unto you has come a new god."

Jack was staring hard at the face. "You're human," he said softly, "flesh and blood like us."

Raymond lowered his arms.

"Brother Jack," he said, "you doubt my divinity? Don't you understand that I have taken on human form to preach the gospel here on earth? Didn't my predecessor take on human form to preach his gospel of meekness and mildness?"

"Yes, but—"

"My father, Starfire the Creator, has sent me to this world to show the truth. If I appeared in my true form, you would be unconvinced. Therefore I have taken on flesh and blood, to be one with you. And I will lead you to great joy and great power and wealth. And in time we shall travel around the world and be greeted everywhere with acclamation; and we shall build great temples to myself and my father, and the world shall know that it is the beginning of a New Time—the New Time of the New God. And now come forward to embrace me and let your hearts be filled with joy. For the world is ours."

Again, he opened his arms. Marcia rather uncertainly walked up to him. He closed his arms around her and kissed her lips, rather hungrily, Jack thought. Certainly it was a flesh-and-blood kiss. When he released her, Marcia was trembling and looking at him with surprise. The god Raymond smiled as she backed away. Then Jeremy stepped forward, and he too was embraced. After he backed away, Raymond turned to Jack.

"My Doubting Thomas." He smiled. "Come forward and greet me, and let your doubts die, for I am what I claim to be."

Jack hesitated a moment. The Raymond of his dreams was so unlike the Raymond of reality—if this *was* reality—he could hardly reconcile the two. In his dreams, Raymond had been fearful, awesome—magical. But now? Despite his pseudo-Biblical way of speaking, Raymond in the flesh had lost his magic. And the strange steel cylinder he had arrived in? Well, it was possible a god might arrive in a steel cylinder, but to Jack the thing looked like a machine—an out-of-this-world machine, true, but a heavenly one? Still, what if he were from another world after all—from a planet revolving around Tau Ceti as Helen's Star Child had claimed to be?

Finally he stepped up to the man. But his mind was more uncertain than ever.

2

Dr. Jan vanderZee sat in the book-lined study and listened with amazement to the thin voice on the cassette. For fifteen minutes he had been listening as the voice described an ingenious theory that combined elements of existing laser-fusion technology with elements of the Russian Tokamak machine system into a stupendously huge fusion reactor called an "infinitron" which, the voice said, could generate directly from the fusion process usable electricity, altogether eliminating the need for conventional power plants. The man in the white-and-gold robe, who had been silently watching him from behind the mahogany desk, got up, crossed the room and turned off the recorder.

"I think you've heard enough to know the information is genuine," he said. "Did you understand the physics?"

"Not all," the Nobel Prize winner replied as he removed his earset. "But enough. You're right. It's not only genuine, it's astounding."

"To you, not to us," Raymond said, closing the recorder cover. "To us, this information is as familiar as atomic physics is to you." He headed back to the desk. They were in the study of Jeremy Bernstein's house. A photograph of Marcia smiled from its silver frame next to the handsome brass desklamp. Raymond sat down and folded his hands on the tooled leather-bound blotter. "The entire cassette has a running time of forty-eight hours," he continued. "We developed a way to miniaturize sound so that an enormous amount of information can be programmed on a small amount of tape. When you listen to the entire tape you'll see that complete details are given not only for the construction of the fusion furnace but also for smaller adaptations that will enable you to build fusion-powered automobiles, planes, trains, home furnaces. . . . Everything you now depend on fossil fuels for, you'll be able to power by cheap, clean fusion power. It will mean a total revolution in your way of life."

Dr. vanderZee stared through his pilot glasses at the extraordinary man across the room from him. The potential of the tape was not as dizzying to him as the presence of Raymond himself.

"Are you really from the future?" he asked.

"Yes. As a physicist, it should hardly surprise you that we finally learned how to travel through time. As you know, it's a dimension, like space. We came to an understanding of the nature of time by studying the black holes in space."

"What possible connection could there be—?"

"Gravity," interrupted Raymond. "But I don't intend to conduct a seminar in advanced physics, doctor. You know that I erased the other cassette Mrs. Bradford brought you in Princeton, and you've been told I arranged DeVoe's death. Do you know why?"

"I have no idea."

"Captain DeVoe intended to give your world his cassette. I intend to sell mine."

"*Sell?* To whom?"

"The highest bidder. My price is ten billion dollars in gold bullion to be deposited at the Crédit Suisse in Zurich one week from today. You see, I have studied your twentieth-century economics—I know where to put the gold. I'd suggest you approach the United States government first." He smiled. "You look surprised, doctor. Don't you believe the cassette is worth ten billion?"

"Easily, but . . . ten billion is more gold than there is in Fort Knox. It would ruin the economy of the country—"

"Nonsense. Your energy costs would be so drastically reduced, your products could undersell the rest of the world and octuple your national income. I really don't care, though, who finally buys the cassette. If Washington refuses, go to the Arabs. They're rich enough."

"But why *me?*" asked vanderZee.

Raymond came around the desk and sat on the edge of it.

"I've chosen you to be my negotiator because you're one of your world's leading physicists, and the heads of government you will approach in my behalf will listen to you. You will not tell them where I am, because I have no illusions about your politicians. Rather than pay my price, they'd kill me to get the information for nothing—if they knew where I was. But I've gone to a great deal of trouble to form my own protective group during the negotiations—it's small, but loyal. And, as I said, you won't tell where I am. I should be reasonably safe."

"How do you know you can trust me?"

"We brought your wife here. We now have her in a safe place. I can assure you she is comfortable, but I can also assure you that if you reveal my whereabouts your wife will die—not pleasantly. I'm something of an expert in that field. However, there's no need for us to be morbid—I'm sure you'll be an excellent negotiator for me. After all, you do want to hear the rest of the cassette, don't you? Curiosity—especially in a scientist—should be a powerful motivation. I take it we understand each other?"

The physicist shook his head. "I don't understand you at all. Why would you sell out your world and our future for ten billion dollars?"

"People have sold out for much less than that, but the answer is simple enough. I have no intention of returning to my world. Even if you manage, with this cassette, to make the skies of the next century turn blue, my world is still an ugly one compared to yours. Years of pollution have devastated the landscape, killed the wild life, the trees, the flowers. I have simple tastes, doctor. I enjoy flowers. . . . I also have some not-so-simple tastes, for which I'll need money. To acquire women, for instance. The women in my world can no longer feel any emotion—fear, pleasure, anything. But your women can at least still experience fear."

"And that excites you?"

"Very much. Our sexuality is as different from yours as our physics. At any rate, I'll need an enormous amount of money to live as I wish . . . to live as a god. When I was chosen to make this time journey, I decided it was a unique opportunity not only to escape my depressing century but to act out the most compelling of all fantasies, the fantasy of divinity. To be an all-powerful being—to be worshiped and feared. . . . Man needs a god to worship and fear, and I am unusually well qualified for the role. Just as you would be if you, with your knowledge, could go back in time to, say, the nineteenth century. The Victorians would worship you because you would know so much more than they. Similarly, your world will worship me . . . because I can work what to it will seem miracles." He took a small metallic globe from the pocket of his robe and held it out in the palm of his right hand. "This device should interest you as a scientist. It was developed in the second decade of the next century for socio-political reasons. It's called a thought projector. When activated, it emits a strong electromagnetic field that enables me to manipulate minds—including yours. In no time at all I could persuade—or terrify—even you into believing anything. For instance . . ."

He depressed a tiny button on the globe and, to

vanderZee's astonishment, he vanished and in his place stood a nude woman—blonde, in her early twenties, with soft skin and lithe figure. She held out her hands. "Don't be afraid, doctor."

"I'm . . . I'm not . . ."

She smiled. "Good. I need to love you, and you to love me. Will you love me, doctor?"

He stared at the lovely apparition as she came from the desk and sat next to him on the leather sofa. She took off his glasses, stuck them in his shirt pocket, held his face between her hands and placed a full kiss on his mouth. He began to respond. He gingerly reached out his hands and put them on her soft, full breasts. At the moment he felt himself becoming erect, she turned into a huge snake that writhed in his hands and hissed in his face.

"Oh God," he yelled. He threw it away from him as he jumped off the sofa. The snake hit the wall and turned into a seven-foot monster that filled the corner of the room. Its head was of a decomposing corpse, its body a mass of writhing pink tentacles. It opened its mouth and gave forth a screech that split the brain. Its hundred tentacles waving like a crazed octopus, it began lumbering across the room toward Dr. vanderZee, emitting its banshee screech. He ran around the desk, grabbed the brass lamp and threw it with all his strength at the monster's head. It passed through the apparition and hit the opposite wall, smashing to the floor.

The creature vanished. In its place stood Raymond, smiling as he held up the thought projector. "You see, it does work."

Dr. vanderZee sank into the desk chair, his hand over his heart, his breath coming in frightened spurts.

"What *was* it?"

"A fantasy from my mind. As were the snake and the girl. That was a brief demonstration, but I think you can see that, in time, I could convince you of anything—or drive you insane."

"Is that what you've done to these people in the house—your so-called followers? Have you driven them insane?"

Raymond replaced the thought projector in the pocket of his robe, and for a moment he seemed less self-assured. "It's possible. I'm afraid one of them already has failed me, but the troopers seem stable enough for the time being."

"What kind of amoral world do you come from where you can treat human beings this way?"

Raymond leaned on the desk. "If you could read the history of your century with our objectivity you'd see you're in no position to preach. With your wars, your Watergates, your love of violence and terror, your greed——"

"I don't deny any of that," interrupted vanderZee, "but there is still some compassion in our world."

"Where?"

"Everywhere. . . . The average American—the average European or Asian or African, for that matter—hates war and violence, wants peace and to banish poverty. We want to save our environment. . . ."

"Then why didn't you *do* it?"

The physicist hesitated. "We're trying. There are groups all over the world that are working to solve these problems. . . ."

"They talk, but they're not effective—and meanwhile, I can assure you, time runs out. What you call your morality wears thinner—your religions, your constitutions, your civilizations all come unstuck. The truth of your world isn't in your pious platitudes or your United Nations resolutions, doctor, as much as you'd like to think so. The truth of your world lies in your corrupt deals, your pornographic theaters, your rapists and muggers and thrill-killers, your egomaniacal Rock idols, your lying politicians' lust for power, your greedy corporations' lust for profits, your angry, uneducated poor and your bored rich. . . . My world is only what your world turned into." His small eyes seemed to penetrate Dr. vanderZee's, and the physicist felt ashamed because he honestly had no retort. "I'm disappointed in you, doctor. You have one of the finest minds of your day, yet you don't have the perception or honesty to look at your world as it really is. No wonder my world became a nightmare. Now get out, you don't interest me any more. Besides, it's late and you need to get an early start for Washington in the morning."

Vanderzee got up from the desk. "What if none of the governments wants to buy?"

"Even politicians shouldn't be that stupid. But if they are . . . well, my time-cylinder has developed another minor mechanical problem, but it's something I can fix soon enough. When I have, I can easily take my cassette a bit further into the future . . . 1984, for instance. By then, your world has developed such a hunger for power-sources that there were thirteen wars in that year alone fought for possession of oil fields, and in one of them a hydrogen bomb was dropped. I have little doubt that in 1984 my cassette will sell. Tell your prospective buyers that I have other markets and am willing to go to them if necessary. That's all, doctor, and remember, I do have your wife."

He crossed the room to the door and opened it, signaling to someone in the living room outside. Jack appeared at the door. Raymond said, "Take Dr. vanderZee to his room. Then prepare your wife for the ceremony."

Jack nodded as the physicist came up to him, looking at him curiously. The two men then went out of the room and Raymond closed the door. They walked in silence across the darkened living room to the stairs and started up. When they reached the second floor, Jack took hold of the physicist's wrist to stop him.

"What," he said quietly, "does the thought projector look like?"

"You listened?"

"Yes. What does it look like?"

"It's a small metal globe. He carries it in his robe."

Jack said nothing for a moment. Then, grimly: "So much for the Great God Raymond."

When the small caravan of police cars returned to Shandy at nine that evening, Helen had been taken by Bixby and Rydell to the deserted campus, then into the school chapel. The troopers led her to its basement and into a storeroom filled with janitorial equipment. Her wrists were handcuffed behind her, her ankles tied with a rope, and a tight gag placed around her mouth. Then the two men left the room, turning out the lights and locking the door. Helen sat down on an unopened carton of detergent and waited in the dark, listening to the drip of a leaky faucet in a mop basin and wondering what further madness awaited her.

After what seemed hours, she heard the key turn in the lock and the door open. The ceiling light was turned on. Marcia was wearing a choir robe Helen recognized as belonging to the school chapel. White plastic daisies were entwined in her black hair to form a virginal diadem. She was carrying a large cardboard dress box from Bergdorf Goodman. The presence of the familiar purple Bergdorf box somehow made her costume seem more bizarre.

"I've come to prepare you," Marcia said, as she hurried over to set down the dress box. She leaned toward Helen, putting her hands on her shoulders.

"*He* made love to me!"

She danced away, twirled around, clutching herself as she hummed a mindless tune. Then she stopped under the light, swaying back and forth like a lazy seaweed in some cosmic dream.

"I am God's mistress," she said. "Isn't that fantastic? Before he arrived, I had my doubts. Jack doubted, too, but Jeremy never lost his faith. But now, no more doubts. You can't imagine how beautiful it was. . . ."

She stopped and pointed across the room. "And it's going to happen to you, too," she said. "Oh yes, it's going to happen to you. . . ."

Humming again, she went to the Bergdorf box, which she'd placed on top of a garbage can, and removed the top. Then she took out a white satin, fur-trimmed evening cloak that looked like something Carole Lombard might have worn in *Twentieth Century*. She held it up for Helen's gagged inspection.

"He told me to find you something appropriate to wear for the ceremony, and I thought of this. It belonged to my mother . . . you'll be beautiful in it, Helen. You know I've always thought you attractive in a sort of dowdy way, but this will make you gorgeous and the Master likes gorgeous women. He told me. He told me *I* was gorgeous . . . I bathed him and massaged him, and he made love to me—oh, God, it was so wonderful. . . . Here, stand up. Try this on."

She carried the cloak over, but Helen remained seated, staring at her. Marcia's face tightened. She kicked Helen's shins, hard. "Stand *up,* dammit!"

Helen, terrified, stood up.

"That's better." She draped the cloak about her shoulders, then stepped back to inspect her. "Not so bad," she said. "And when we fix the bridal veil . . ."

The *bridal veil?* Just as the insanity of what apparently awaited her began to penetrate Helen's consciousness, the building rumbled with distant organ music. Marcia looked up at the ceiling. "I wonder who's playing for the ceremony?" she asked. "Sarah Blake's in Vermont. Who could Raymond have gotten at two in the morning? . . ." She looked back at Helen. "Of course. How stupid of me. He can do anything." She returned to the Bergdorf box to take out a bridal veil and hairbrush. "Can you imagine," she went on in a chatty tone, "Norton Akroyd's disappeared. No one knows why, and the Master's upset. . . . Norton was one of his favorites. . . ." She returned to Helen and began brushing her hair. "Who would *want* to run away from the Master? Oh Helen, you have no idea how fabulous my life's going to be from now on. He told me all about it while he made love to me. . . . We're going to be rich, fantastically rich! He's funding the Church with billions and then we're going to travel all over the world and spread the Gospel and set up temples to Starfire. . . . It'll be just a bit of a change in the old life-style, won't it? To get out of *this* dreary burg. . . . We'll be . . ." she thought a moment, then whispered, "Stars."

She put down the brush and picked up the bridal veil. As she positioned it in Helen's hair, she leaned close to her face and smiled.

"But *you,*" she said, "you're the luckiest one of all because *you're* going to be the bride of Raymond."

She stepped back and looked at Helen, draped in her satin cloak and crowned with her white tulle veil that flowed down over her gagged mouth and disbelieving eyes.

"Very nice. And don't worry, Helen. I'll look after Jack when you're gone. After all, I've looked after him before." She laughed. "In the River View Motel, that is. Did you ever guess? Did you know he and I had been lovers? No, I don't think you guessed . . . you're too naïve, too dumb. Well, it doesn't make any difference now. . . ."

The door opened and Sergeant Bixby stepped into the room.

"We're ready," he said.

"So are we."

The trooper pulled a jackknife from his pocket and cut Helen's ankle rope.

"All right, Mrs. Bradford, we're going upstairs."

Helen tried to reassure herself that this was another hallucinating dream, that soon she would wake up, except that lately the dreams had merged into the terrifying reality. Marcia grabbed her arm and pushed her toward the door.

"Don't be nervous," she said. "It's going to be a *spectacular* wedding. You'll see."

Helen stumbled out of the room into the basement of the chapel. The chapel basement. Ben's cellar. The love-death.

Oh God, she thought, has the whole world gone mad?

3

The organ pealed the majestic opening chords of Sigfrid Karg-Elert's chorale prelude, "Now Thank We All Our God"—except there was no visible organist at the console. The chapel was empty as the strange processional began moving down the aisle toward the altar. First came Jeremy Bernstein in a white choir robe, carrying a bowl of smoking incense. Behind him was Jack, also robed, holding a lighted candle. Then Marcia, carrying the white-feathered owl head that Ben Scovill had worn when he loved and sent to her death Judy Siebert. After Marcia came the "bride," still bound and gagged, but the gag and the handcuffs were almost concealed by the wedding veil and the white cloak. She was flanked by the two young troopers, Highet and Rydell; behind her, holding a gun pointed at the base of her spine, was Sergeant Bixby.

There were no lights in the chapel. The place was illuminated by the great blue flame that flared from the center of the altar like a giant gas jet. Helen told herself it had to be an illusion, like the illusions of her dreams. She told herself it was Raymond, flooding all their minds with his lurid images—except she was no longer sure. Perhaps she was in the presence of God. Certainly the sight of the flame was awesome. She was afraid but actually felt a sense of primitive reverence that defied all her logic—the overwhelming music, the bombarde rumbling of the deep dominant pedal G that shook the church to its foundations, the magical flame. . . . Mustn't the presence of God be *something* like this, after all? Majestic? Frightening? Beautiful?

As the music reached its massive climax, the procession halted in front of the flame. The music stopped, its echoes bounding with dying energy around the building until all was silence.

Then the skull appeared in the middle of the flame, high over them, and a voice filled their ears.

"I am Starfire the Creator," intoned the voice. "And I have sent my son, the god Raymond, into your midst. Tremble and worship. As my son is life, he is also death. As he is joy, he is also corruption. Let those who would challenge his power beware, for the anger of Starfire reaches beyond the grave . . . there is a cold and distant star where they shall be sent, guarded by monsters of unsurpassed evil, and their fate eclipses the maddest ravings of your feeble minds. So beware! And believe! And it is I who tell you this— I, Starfire, the Creator! Starfire—God!"

The Voice died and the skull faded from view as the blue flame dwindled swiftly down to a tiny glow, then vanished. Simultaneously, a new light sprang up from the floor of the altar: a white light that threw its illumination upward onto the figure of Raymond. He was standing on the altar, dressed in his white robe, his arms stretched wide. In his right palm he held the small metallic globe—the thought projector.

"Bring forth the Bride of Raymond," he cried.

The blue flame and the Voice might have been illusions, but Helen had no illusions about what awaited her. The logically insane climax to the dreams and Raymond's logically insane religion was her marriage to Raymond in an ultimate love-death. Ultimate, at least for her. The Bride of Raymond. The Bride of Frankenstein. Again she was living a horror film, this time apparently in reality rather than in dream. She told herself she must not show fear. She remembered the dream scene in the Coupling Room when Raymond had complained about his victim's lack of fear and how he hungered for an emotional response. Well, she would give him no satisfaction.

The troopers were now pushing her toward the altar. She passed Jack. He was watching her impassively. Was it possible that only a short while ago they were a reasonably happy married couple? Or were they? Had her happiness been another illusion? Illusion, and reality? Perhaps reality was illusion.

As she climbed onto the altar and was jerked toward her bridegroom, her eyes focused on the shiny metal globe in his hand. Now it seemed to emit a light of its own, a white light which mesmerized her. Another illusion? And what was the globe? She found herself becoming lost in the light until it filled her vision. She could no longer see Raymond or the troopers pulling her toward him or the church or the celebrants.

All she saw was the light.

And then she found herself back in the glowing white marble bedroom of the previous dream, and the soft opening strains of the "Liebestod" filled her ears. She was once again sitting in the gigantic bed; as in the dream, she was wearing a gossamer white robe. Through the arch stepped another white robe. Raymond. He stood at the foot of the bed.

"I've been planning this," he said. "Ever since you killed my first apostle, Ben."

"I killed Ben because he would have killed me," she replied. "You turned him into a murderer."

He was moving around the foot of the bed.

"Ben made the decision to kill. I suggested, never ordered. When he killed, though, he was bound to me forever."

"He wouldn't have killed if you hadn't suggested it."

"Perhaps. Who knows? Your husband killed you in 1977. Dr. Akroyd was right. We are all potential murderers. Man isn't a potential saint; he's a potential monster."

"That's only a half-truth. Your whole disgusting so-called religion is made up of half-truths."

He was beside her now, and sat down next to her on the bed.

"Aren't all religions?" he said, examining her face and her throat.

"Why didn't you try to suggest killing to me?" she asked.

"Because I knew DeVoe was in your mind, and I didn't want him to know what I was doing. I let him show you the truth about us because it didn't matter—he was about to die, just as you are." He paused. "And you are going to die in fear."

"In fear of death, perhaps. Not of you."

He put his hand on her bare arm and smiled.

"The brave Mrs. Bradford, who has been so staunch in the face of the infinite."

"That woman in the Coupling Room—the prisoner. She wasn't afraid of you."

"Her mind had been destroyed by the prison officials. We destroy all criminal minds so that they feel neither hate nor fear. The problem is they become emotional neuters. But your mind hasn't been destroyed—yet."

"Until it is, I won't fear you. I did once, but not any more. I pity you."

"Pity a god?"

"You can't love."

"How Jesuitical," he said. "I rather admire it. But love and beauty are dead concepts in my world, just as they are dying ones in yours. The only honest emotion we can feel is terror, and the joy of inflicting terror—which can be more satisfying than love. Love never lasts. But the love-*death* lasts forever."

As he said it, the "Liebestod" swelled and he leaned forward and kissed her mouth. She felt revulsion but was powerless to resist him. And then the light flooded her mind again for a moment so that she was blinded; but when the light ebbed, she found herself lying naked on the bed. When she saw what was on top of her, making love to her, the scream echoed through her mind and pains of terror shot through her chest.

Holding her in its arms, its body thrusting its grotesque haunches, its face inches from hers, its yellow eyeballs staring into her soul, was the moldering thing that had come into her bedroom that night after Jeremy had left the house and she had heard Jack coming up the stairs. And now she began to see what Raymond meant, for the horror that poured through her was electrifying, and the revulsion she felt so fierce it became almost fulfilling. And she saw the face of madness, and of death.

The light flooded her brain again. When it receded she found herself on the chapel altar. Raymond was standing in front of her in his white robe, smiling as he lifted the bridal veil from her face and removed the gag from her mouth.

"You fear me *now*. You fear me now."

She was transfixed.

"Remove her handcuffs."

She felt the steel clasps release her wrists behind her, and she brought her aching arms around in front, instinctively putting up her hands to push him off.

It was then the shot rang out, its report echoing around the chapel. She watched as the face so close to her twisted with pain. She was aware of something reddish-gray spurting from his head, just above his right ear, and she heard him grunt as he fell forward. He was a big man. His heaviness nearly brought her to the altar floor with him, but she managed to get out from under him. He hit the wooden floor with a thud and lay still.

The light vanished. The chapel was in darkness except for Jack's candle. She heard something metallic bounce down the altar steps, and wondered if it was the globe he had held in his hand.

"Turn on the lights." It was Jack's voice, and the mundane order seemed to bring reality rushing back into the vacuum of Raymond's fantasies.

"Where are they?" Bixby called out.

"In the robing room, off the altar."

No one spoke as Bixby bumped his way through the dark to the door of the robing room. Then the distant flick of electric switches as the chapel lights turned on.

He was lying in blood. He was dead. She stared at the body, as did the young trooper beside her, who looked dazed. Marcia Bernstein ran up to the altar and knelt down beside Raymond. Tears were running down her cheeks as she said, "He's dead! Our God is dead!"

"He wasn't God," said Jack, and Helen realized he was holding the Smith & Wesson. He was coming toward the altar, and Marcia stood up.

"That's not true. He *was* God, and he was beautiful——"

"He was a fraud," shouted Jack, picking up the thought projector from under a pew. "A fraud who used us with *this*. This thing, this metal globe caused all the dreams, all the terror, all the"—he waved his hand toward the chapel ceiling—"blue flames and skulls and Starfire voices and special effects. . . ." He ran up the altar steps, putting the thought projector into his pocket. "Raymond turned us into killers because he needed stooges, not apostles. He turned Bixby and Highet and Rydell into kidnappers because he wanted a private army, not a congregation." He turned to Helen. "I heard Raymond talking to vander-Zee."

She took off the bridal veil and the white-satin cloak, and there was a flicker of hope in her tired eyes.

"Then you killed him to save me?"

"You can believe that if it makes you feel better."

He addressed the others. "I killed him to save *us*. Because, if Raymond isn't God, we're not above the law. And I don't believe any judge is going to let us off because we say our minds were zapped by a man from the twenty-first century. If we don't get life, we'll end up in a padded cell. But now we can avoid both."

"How?" said Bixby.

"If there are no bodies, there are no murders. We can put Raymond and Ben and the others in the time-cylinder up on the mountain and send them all forward into the next century. Meanwhile, we've got the cassette. There's nothing stopping us from doing what Raymond was going to do—sell it for ten billion, divide the money and——"

"What cassette?" a confused Jeremy asked.

"I'll explain later. Take my word: it's worth far more than Fort Knox. How about it? If you're rich, you don't need a god."

Helen watched their faces. They were rising to the bait. After a moment, Bixby said, "But who knows how to work the cylinder?"

"I do," said Helen quietly.

They all turned to look at her.

"I was shown by Captain DeVoe, the other tempo-naut."

"I sure as hell don't know what a temponaut is," said Bixby, "but I'm game to get rich. Come on, let's get him out of here."

Jack took off his choir robe and dropped it onto the floor. Then he and the troopers picked up the body of the fallen god and carried him off the altar as Marcia Bernstein wiped the blood from the floor.

4

The cassette. There was only one thing that was important to her now, the cassette. The love-deaths, the mad pretensions of Raymond, her own safety—all were insignificant compared to the information on the tape. If God was in nature, then the ultimate blasphemy was not Raymond's posturings but a future earth befouled by the swirling clouds of pollution she had seen in the dream. The earth had to be saved.

The threat now was not Raymond but the greed of her husband and the others. The promise of untold wealth had infected them as swiftly as Raymond's preverse religion had. She had seen the fear on their faces replaced by greed as they listened to Jack. What if the government balked—or haggled? Governments were greedy too. What if they sent in troops to take the cassette rather than pay billions? It was possible. And in the ensuing mêlée who would be thinking of the future, who would protect the cassette? It would be burned, destroyed, lost. . . .

Nothing else mattered but the cassette.

The funeral march up the dark mountain was in its way as bizarre as the scene in the chapel. One by one the bodies were removed from their coffins in Ben's cellar, hauled up the stairs to the kitchen, taken outside, then carried up the hill to the time-cylinder, where they were taken inside and dumped unceremoniously on the floor. She saw that the bodies were still remarkably preserved, considering that they had not been embalmed; and as she stood in front of the black time-window watching Ben and the others being aligned along the banquette, she shuddered. But there was no time to respect the dead. They had to be hustled away, shuttled out of the ocean of time into another age in order to save the living.

At one point, when she was alone in the metallic compartment, she went to the side of the time-window and opened the control panel. She set the time-dials and moved the red switch to "on." Then she closed the panel again and resumed her position in front of the window.

The last body to be brought aboard was Doug, the truck driver. Then Jack, who was sweating from the exertion, looked at his wife and said, "Now what? How does the thing work?"

She looked around the small room. Sergeant Bixby and the two young troopers, Highet and Rydell. Jeremy and Marcia. Jack. All watching her.

"I have to go to the compartment below," she said. "The controls are there. You wait here. Then we'll all leave together."

She made her way through the living, and the dead, to the ladder, then started to climb down.

"Wait a minute," said Jack in a puzzled tone. "What compartment below? I didn't see any . . ."

Her eyes were just above the floor level, and she saw the look of fear come over his face.

"Good-by, Jack," she said. Then she disappeared down the ladder.

"For God's sake, stop her—"

She could hear the panic, *feel* it, as she stepped outside the time-cylinder and unlatched the open door.

Then the screams, the sound of someone scrambling down the ladder—

She slammed the door shut.

The tall steel cylinder began to dematerialize.

And then she was left alone on top of the mountain, with nothing but a soft breeze rustling the needles of the pines.

EPILOGUE

Death and
Transfiguration

1

She returned to the campus in her Toyota, went to the Bernstein house and unlocked Dr. vanderZee from the second-floor bedroom. Then she told him what she had done.

"You *murdered* them?"

"No. I got rid of them long enough for you to take the cassette away from here. I set the time dials for two days from now. The cylinder will return at eight in the morning the day after tomorrow. My husband killed Raymond so *he* could sell the cassette, but it's too important to be sold. It has to be given to the world, the way DeVoe intended. Once there's a price on it, God knows what might happen to it."

Dr. vanderZee considered this for a moment, then, to her delight, agreed she had probably acted wisely. "But what about their safety?" he asked. "Is there enough oxygen in the cylinder for them?"

"It goes five years per earth day, so one earth month is only twenty-four minutes cylinder time, and two earth days is less than two minutes. They'll be all right for two minutes. And if it gives them a good scare, that won't hurt them either. Do you have any idea where the cassette is?"

"It was downstairs in the study. He left it on the recorder. But where's my wife?"

She started down the stairs.

"I saw a light in Beline Hall. They probably locked her in the lab. Let's get the cassette first. . . ."

But it was gone. They searched the study, and then the rest of the house, but the cassette was nowhere to be found. Helen said they should try the chapel next, but Dr. vanderZee, understandably worried about his wife, went first to the psychology building, where, in fact, they found Mrs. vanderZee asleep on the bed in the lab. They hadn't harmed her, though she was totally at a loss as to what was happening. Her husband and Helen explained as they went next door to the chapel and searched it for the cassette. Finally, just before dawn, Helen gave up. "He must have had it with him." She sighed. "In the pocket of his robe. Since everything depended on the cassette, he probably wanted to keep it with him."

"Then we'll have to wait for the cylinder to return?" asked Dr. vanderZee.

Helen nodded wearily.

"I guess so. Damn it, it never occurred to me he might have kept it with him."

They were standing on the altar, and she looked down at the blood stain on the floor. Raymond had outmaneuvered her, even in death. Raymond, the man who had presumed to be God, who had died a mortal's death. She wondered at the monstrous fantasies in his mind. Was it possible that the same human race that built the medieval cathedrals could build such a perverse, sordid, hideous world as the world she had seen in the dreams? She had accused him of preaching half-truths about the nature of man, but perhaps she had been fooling herself. After all, he had unleashed monsters in the minds of her husband and the Bernsteins and Norton . . . monsters she would never have believed existed had she not seen the shrine filled with their victims. Perhaps he had been right after all. . . .

"What are you thinking about?" asked Dr. vander-Zee.

"Raymond," she said, looking up. "Is it possible he was what we're becoming?"

"He told me his world is what our world turned into," said vanderZee. "I don't *like* to believe him, but I wonder if I don't have to."

"But won't the information on the cassette change the future?" asked his wife.

"It may change the outer pollution," said Helen, "but what about the inner?"

She looked up at the chapel ceiling and saw in her mind the blue flame and heard the voice of Starfire. The monstrous ego-mania, the perversion, the love of violence, the violence of love: she knew they were part of her world. What she hated to accept was the idea that they were the part that would survive and, ultimately, triumph.

It was decided that the vanderZees, though they were both exhausted, would borrow Jack's Volvo and drive back to Princeton. Dr. vanderZee wanted to alert his colleagues at the Plasma Physics Laboratory to the fantastic treasure trove of information that was about to be theirs: for not only was there the unlocked secret of controlled thermonuclear fusion on the cassette, there was the marvel of the thought projector (which Helen remembered seeing Jack put in his pocket) as well as the miracle of the time-cylinder itself. He would return to Shandy the following evening with his three assistants and several other members of the science faculty who would be as eager to examine the time-cylinder as himself. Then, the next morning, they would accompany Helen to the top of the mountain to await the return of the cylinder and its occupants.

What to do with them remained an enigma. The question of their guilt was at best tricky—would they, in fact, have killed if it hadn't been for Raymond? And yet, of course, they *had* killed. Moreover, there was the problem of Jack's stealing the cassette, though in the two minutes they would be sealed in the cylinder they probably wouldn't discover the cassette was with them. Still, Jack had his gun, the troopers had theirs, and it was doubtful they would have changed their minds about selling the tape. For that reason, Dr. vanderZee wanted to have police on the mountaintop to force them to give up the cassette. Helen didn't agree. "Jack's afraid," she said as the vanderZees got into the Volvo. "He's committed murder, and now he doesn't have Raymond to protect him. If he sees the police when he gets out of the cylinder, he might panic and start firing. I think we should try to convince them that they have to give themselves up. Now that you and Mrs. vanderZee can back up their story, and with the time-cylinder there as proof it all really happened"—she liked saying that; it made her feel much better—"there should be a good chance at some kind of reduced sentence."

"Perhaps," said vanderZee, "though they're going to need an awfully good lawyer. But you're wrong about the police. We must have them there so they can see the cylinder materialize, which is the best way to convince them. And I don't think we can take any chances with your husband: the cassette's too important. What if he uses his gun on us if the police aren't there?"

Helen considered this, reluctantly gave in.

"All right. Tomorrow night after you get here, we'll go to the state police. I don't think it's wise, but I suppose we have no choice."

"Good."

VanderZee started the car, then looked through the open window at Helen. "Are you going to divorce him?" he asked.

"I don't know."

"You couldn't feel the same about him after what's happened."

"No, I don't feel the same. But . . ." She was thinking that perhaps, with Raymond dead, the destructive influence he had on Jack's personality might die also. Or was that wishful thinking? Could the murders be erased? Could the unleashed monster in his mind ever be locked up again?

"We'll see," she said, and the physicist changed the subject. Telling her he'd see her the next evening, he turned the Volvo around and drove off, leaving her standing alone in front of the white house on the side of the mountain.

He was halfway to New York before he remembered.

"Oh my God."

"What's wrong?" his wife said, seated next to him.

"The time-cylinder. Raymond told me there was something wrong with it."

"What?"

"I don't know. He said he could fix it easily enough, but . . ." He hesitated. "Perhaps I'm too anxious. If it was able to dematerialize, it presumably is operating correctly. . . ."

He said nothing more as he headed the Volvo south on Route 684 toward White Plains. Forty-five minutes later he crossed the George Washington Bridge, passing the early morning commuter traffic going the other way. Then he started toward the Jersey Turnpike.

Anthony di Giorgio was nervous about the wind shift.

He stood on the edge of his fifteen-acre dump outside Elizabeth, New Jersey, and watched the black smoke roiling up from the burning garbage. Anthony's passion for pasta and wine had girdled him with a hundred extra pounds in the thirty years since he had returned from the Second World War a slim, bemedaled ex-Seabee. Now, in his flowered, open-neck sportshirt and gray slacks, he looked as chunky as his bank balance. For Anthony was rich. Starting with a small junk business financed by his wartime shipboard poker winnings, Anthony had grown, acquiring apartment buildings and dumps along his road to riches until he was able to buy the biggest prize of all: a fleet of garbage trucks. Anthony fed off the waste of the world, and he flourished.

He was proud of his success, proud of his gray Fleetwood, his $200,000 house in Short Hills, his summer house at Sea Girt, his plump, pretty wife Carla, his three handsome sons and two beautiful daughters. Just the previous June his elder daughter, Isabelle, had been married to the son of a loan-business executive (which was the somewhat misleading description of his profession given in the papers) and the reception, held at one of the poshest country clubs in New Jersey, had been spectacular. Anthony still glowed as he recalled the guest list, which included three congressmen, an ex-Governor, four mayors, a pride of aldermen, a celebrated golf pro, at least a dozen millionaires, several starlets. . . . It had been a glittering showcase of his success, flashing his wealth and influence to the world. It had been a smash.

Of course, Anthony had problems, not the least annoying of which were the damned antipollution laws the local ecology freaks had managed to push through City Hall. Nutty housewives, weirdo egghead types, hippies, fairies, Commies—that was how Anthony thought of the clean-air shitheads, as he called them. Against burning garbage . . . Christ, garbage had been burned for centuries, hadn't it? They wanted him to bulldoze the garbage into the earth: did they have any idea how much bulldozers cost? Besides, it wasn't practical. The water table was too high. Hadn't he even hired a goddam expert from New York to write a paper proving that if he buried the garbage it might seep into the water supply and poison the local wells? It didn't do any good, though. The clean-air shitheads wouldn't listen to reason. They had a bug up their ass. Clean air . . . well, he wasn't against clean air, but why didn't they go after the real polluters, the utilities and factories? Why pick on him? All he was doing was burning a little garbage, for Chrissake. . . .

He had managed to get around the ordinances, in a way. He knew the right people—they had all been to his daughter's reception, hadn't they?— and the right contribution quietly made to the right political club had worked its usual magic. Certain changes had been written into the antipollution ordinance. Under certain weather conditions, dumps in certain areas would be allowed to burn garbage . . . and needless to say, Anthony di Giorgio's dumps just happened to lie in the specified areas. The clean-air shitheads had yelled their heads off, but this time they didn't get anywhere. People were getting tired of all the fuss. Besides, unlike Anthony, they weren't smart enough to make those quiet little political donations that worked the quiet magic.

So yesterday they had started burning garbage, because yesterday the weather conditions were right. The wind had been from the west, blowing the black smelly smoke out toward the ocean. But this morning, at dawn, the wind had lazily swung around to the east, and now the smoke was billowing the wrong way over the Jersey Turnpike, and Anthony di Giorgio was nervous. If the damned wind didn't shift soon, the Turnpike Authority would start howling, and that could mean real trouble. How often did they get an easterly wind? he would explain. Hardly ever, and he had no way of knowing . . . but it would be sticky. The Turnpike Authority had a real bug up its ass about fogs and smoke and reduced visibility on the giant road with its heavy truck traffic. If the wind didn't shift soon, they'd be on his neck. . . .

He was watching the road now, about three hundred yards from where he was standing. The constant distant roar of the Diesels lessened as they braked before plunging into the smoke. Anthony judged that by now a third of a mile was being affected. If only the

goddam wind would shift! Of all the fucking luck . . .
the rest of the sky without a cloud, and there, for
everyone to see, di Giorgio's smog. . . . And the worst
part was, the smoke was getting thicker. Christ, you
probably couldn't see twenty feet in that mess. He was
sure as hell glad his limousine wasn't in there; it could
be hairy. The T.A. will be calling any minute, yelling
their heads off. . . . Well, it wasn't *his* fault. He
couldn't control the goddam wind.

It was then he heard the screech of brakes, followed
by a slamming crash. He winced and strained his ears.
Momentary silence, then the bellow of a Diesel horn,
the screeching of more brakes, another crash. Two,
three . . . how many more? Oh Christ, there'd be hell
to pay. . . . He started running toward his Cadillac. He
had to get to the office, start making phone calls, call
the mayor, call his lawyer . . .

Just as he reached his car, he heard still another
horn blast, this one squeakily weak, like a Volkswagen
or one of those foreign jobs. Then another crash.

If it's one of those little cars, they'll have to take the
driver out with a blotter, he thought.

He got into his car, slammed the door, started the
engine and roared away from the dump, heading for
his office and the telephone.

2

Helen heard the news on the radio.

The vanderZees had been her best hope with the police as well as her one link to what she still thought of as normality. Now that they were dead—killed in a brutal, senseless multiple accident on the Jersey Turnpike—she could do nothing but sit in her living room and stare out the window. What should she do now? Should she go to the police as Dr. vanderZee had insisted? But if there was to be any chance of reestablishing her old relationship with her husband, it would be blasted forever if, when they stepped out of the time-cylinder, they were met by a phalanx of armed state troopers summoned by her. She could imagine the look of hatred Jack would give her—yes, she had ample evidence he already hated her, but Raymond was dead now and there was that chance (slim, true) that the old Jack would return, and she had loved the old Jack, enough that she couldn't bring herself to destroy the chance.

Yet not to summon the police was taking an enormous risk. Could she handle Jack by herself? He and the others would come out of the cylinder not realizing that two days rather than two minutes had elapsed, and she would be there trying to convince them it was all over and they must give themselves up to the police. . . . What if Jack told her to go to hell? Ten billion dollars was an incredible amount of money, after all. And Marcia, already on the fringe of madness—could she be reasoned with? And the troopers, ready to become instant millionaires, would they be willing to hand themselves over to their peers for probable lengthy jail sentences?

And there was herself. She, too, had killed. Could she *prove* self-defense? (After all, she might be called a jealous wife.) Was she anxious to go to jail if she couldn't prove it? Hardly.

She wandered around the empty house the rest of the day trying to come to a decision, and failing. She couldn't eat and, though she was exhausted, she couldn't sleep. Once she looked in the bathroom mirror and saw the dark circles under her bloodshot eyes and realized, with a sense of shock, that the hideous experience she had lived through had aged her. She no longer looked a healthy twenty-eight but rather a weary, frantic woman on the verge of middle-age, which didn't do much for her spirits. She was fighting the ghost of Ben as well as Raymond—and Jack no longer finding her physically attractive? Jack, Jack . . . she wanted him, ached for him, wished he were there now to make love to her, to tell her he loved her and that love was not dead in the world and to stop the nightmare.

At six she turned on the television and watched the news. A young woman had been brutally stabbed to death in Greenwich Village and the police were looking for her murderer. Violence, the nightly violence that thought-projected into millions of living rooms. Was there never an end to it? The Connecticut State Police had issued a five-state alarm for three troopers who had disappeared. Disappeared? They had vanished into thin air. Literally, she thought. Then a special report on the wave of disappearances that had plagued northwest Connecticut. Mr. Fredericks of Fairfax was interviewed in his house as he fed his motherless son. Mr. Fredericks, looking gaunt, said he still hoped to find his wife. . . . Hope? He was a fool to hope. She was dead. She was lying on the floor of the time-cylinder, whirling somewhere outside of time.

Helen could stand no more. She got up and switched channels. On her screen appeared a tangled mass of crumpled steel, and she thought she recognized Jack's Volvo crushed between a Diesel and a pickup truck. Then on the screen flashed a photograph of Dr. vanderZee, smiling behind his pilot glasses as the newscaster's voice, unemotionally statistical, announced the death of the eminent physicist.

She heard herself screaming. She wanted to destroy the news. Taking up a crystal ashtray, she threw it with all her strength at the television. It crashed through the tube, and the set flashed fire and fragmented with an explosion. Silence and smoke.

She was shaking, her mind reeling. Stumbling out of the house, she ran onto the lawn and fell in the grass. She lay there, crying softly, as the evening sky blazed pink and gold and blue above her. It took her nearly ten minutes to quiet down. Then she got up and wearily returned to the house.

She stared at the shattered television set. She had to hang on, *had* to. She wouldn't go to pieces now, too much depended on her. She had to hang on.

Twenty minutes later, a police car pulled into the driveway and parked in front of the house. Two troopers got out and walked toward the front door as Helen watched fearfully from a window. When she answered the door, the first trooper asked if Mr. Bradford was home.

"No," she answered. "I'm Mrs. Bradford. What did you want to see him about?"

"Where is your husband?"

Tell him, she thought. Now's your chance. *Tell* him! Everything!

"He's . . . away."

Away? My God, *is* he!

"Is anything wrong?" she went on.

"Well, there was a bad accident in New Jersey this morning . . ."

"Yes, I heard about it."

"And the Jersey police contacted us. It seems that one of the cars involved was registered in your husband's name."

"That's right. I lent it to Dr. vanderZee and his wife. I feel terrible about what happened."

Tell them the truth, her mind screamed. But her mouth lied.

"Yes, it was a real mess. Ten people killed. Was Dr. vanderZee a close friend?"

"No—that is, he had come up here for . . . for professional reasons."

"Oh. Well, anyway, we wanted to notify you, and let you know that you'll be getting a copy of the accident report in a few days. Your husband will need that for the insurance."

"Thank you, I'll tell him."

The trooper smiled and touched his cap.

"I guess that's all. Good evening."

"Good evening."

The two men returned to the car and as they drove down the drive she closed the front door and leaned against it. Now the decision was made. She had her chance. She wouldn't go to the police. She couldn't.

She would go up the mountain alone.

During the next thirty-six hours she didn't leave the house. She sealed herself in, munched crackers and cheese, drank wine, waited. The house was filled with ghosts; she was beginning to hate it. At one point she dozed off in her chair in the living room, and when she awoke she was convinced Raymond was in the kitchen. She forced herself to go through the dining room to look. The kitchen was empty, but she remembered the aura and the refrigerator filled with writhing snakes and she began to sweat. And then the vision of Jack and Ben making love, with Roger the hitchhiker hanging lifeless from the cellar beam. . . . She forced herself to go to the refrigerator and open it. No snakes, only a half-empty quart of milk, the cheese, some aging grapes, a bottle of Chablis. She took the wine back to the living room, refilled her glass, waited.

At seven-thirty on the morning they were to return, she left the house and started up the mountain. It was a gray, cool day that held the first hint of autumn. She had put on a sweater. She was tense, apprehensive. She was also glad the wait was nearly over. Whatever Jack's reaction to her plea to turn themselves in might be, she was longing to see him, longing to touch him. The house with its ghosts had become an unendurable prison.

She arrived at the top of the mountain at fifteen minutes before eight, and sat down on a tree-stump to await the final quarter hour. She looked at the cloudy sky and remembered the auditorium of the future with its dome holding out the lethal pollution. When the time-cylinder reappeared with the body of DeVoe, would they try again to visit the past and dispatch someone else back into time? They wouldn't have to if she was successful. She had to be successful, had to get the cassette.

The minutes dragged. Finally, at one minute before eight, she stood up. What would they say when they stepped out of the cylinder? What would *she* say?

She looked at her watch. Eight. She tensed, waiting for the magic to happen.

Nothing.

Maybe her watch was fast.

Five minutes passed, still nothing. Her watch wasn't *that* fast. She began to wonder if she had the wrong day. . . . No. Impossible. She had been very exact when she set the time dials, and she had checked twice. There could be no mistake.

Had Raymond done something to the cylinder before he left it? Perhaps, but that seemed unlikely.

Had *they* done something to the controls? Locked in

the macabre compartment, finding themselves sealed in with the corpses, had they panicked, found the control panel and done something to the dials. No, that was impossible too. She remembered what Captain De-Voe had told her: once the journey started, nothing could change it.

Then where *were* they? It was eight-fifteen.

"Jack—?"

She said it aloud, realizing she was talking to the wind, but becoming so frightened she didn't care.

"I am Starfire, the Creator."

She heard the echoing voice in her mind.

"There is a cold and distant star, guarded by monsters of unsurpassed evil . . ."

She clapped her hands over her ears to keep the voice out, even though she knew it was an empty gesture. Was it possible Starfire had destroyed them all for destroying his son Raymond? Crazy . . . Starfire didn't exist, Raymond wasn't a god. . . . She mustn't think this way, she must hang on. . . .

Eighty-twenty. Still nothing.

She envisioned the tiny metallic compartment filled with corpses. . . . No, not *all* corpses yet. Jack was still alive, gaunt, ravening, feeding on what was left of Marcia Bernstein as her blood ran down his chin and the time-cylinder hurtled through eternity. . . .

"JACK. Oh God, where *are* you?"

Was it possible . . . the malfunction. Something had gone wrong with Raymond's ship when he started the journey. Was it possible the malfunction had repeated?

It was then she saw Star Child.

She stared across the clearing. He was standing under one of the large pines looking like a Botticelli angel, a sweet smile on his sweet face, his hair gold, his tunic spotless white . . . an angel. How stupid she was not to have realized that at the very beginning! He was her personal angel, her guardian angel! After all, they had had Raymond and Starfire. Didn't she deserve at least an angel? Of course she did.

"Star Child," she called, running across the clearing toward him. "Where are they? What's happened to them?"

"They're at peace," he said.

"I didn't mean to kill them. Oh God, I didn't *mean* to . . ."

"You must not feel guilt."

"Mustn't I?" Her voice was like a little girl's, uncertain, hopeful . . . "But Jack . . . I loved Jack so much. Do you think he still loved me, or had he become . . . like Raymond?"

"You must not grieve for him. He had become like Raymond. They were all bad, but you are good."

She smiled as the tears began running down her cheeks. "Yes, I am, aren't I?" She suddenly tensed and looked around, her eyes darting suspiciously. "Is Raymond here? And Starfire? They're bad too, aren't they?"

"Very bad. But they won't harm you. I've come to protect you. I'll be with you forever. I'll keep the evil people away. . . . I'll protect you from all your fears and worries. You will be safe with me."

Her tenseness vanished. She was filled with serenity. She knelt before the beautiful child and kissed his hand.

"How I love you, Star Child," she said. "How glad I am you've come back. Do you promise you'll never leave me?"

"I promise."

She stood up, still holding his hand.

"My angel," she said happily. "My very own angel. I think I've always wanted one and didn't really know it. Shall we go home?"

He smiled his beautiful smile and together, hand in hand, they started down the mountain to her house.

3

Almost any psychiatrist would have diagnosed Helen's problem as the beginning of paranoia. She had the classic symptoms: suspicion of a plot against her, inability to differentiate between reality and fantasy, a brooding, building sense of physical danger and terror, a confusion of sex with violence. Paranoia (from the Greek for "beside the mind") was the twentieth-century madness; it reached into the White House, corporate board rooms, churches, art museums, terrorist hide-outs and rock concerts. Was it any wonder it reached into the mind of a Connecticut housewife as well?

But Norton Akroyd wasn't just any psychiatrist, and he knew that, for Helen Bradford, Raymond made all the difference. What might be paranoia in others was in Helen's case the devastating result of the Master's power to invade and control minds. Sometimes Norton wondered if *he* weren't losing his hold on reality, even wondered if the Master—the god Raymond—weren't really a manifestation of his own powers . . . but then his good sense and faith would reassert themselves and he would know that the miracle of a new God was actually occurring and that such thoughts were dangerous and, indeed, presumptuous. Also terrifying.

His faith was strong when he had stalked the woman

down West Eighth Street in Greenwich Village through the nighttime crowd of hippies, hookers and tourists to the corner of Sixth Avenue. There she had headed uptown, and he followed. She wasn't aware of him; he was just part of the crowd. Passing Balducci's Market, she had turned east on Eleventh Street and started toward Fifth Avenue. Perhaps she became aware of him then, because the lovely street, with its nine-teenth-century houses (marred only by the blank where a few years earlier one of the loveliest houses had been blown to eternity by college-age Weather-men building bombs in the basement), was as empty as Eighth Street had been crowded. But she didn't turn to look at the owner of the clicking Gucci heels behind her, even though it was almost midnight. She kept walking until she heard the footsteps break into a run. It was only then she turned to see the well-dressed man with the knife in his hand, watched almost with detachment as he plunged it twice into her stomach. As she staggered toward the stoop of a brownstone, still disbelieving it was happening to her, the man ran past her toward Fifth Avenue and disappeared into the night.

As Norton drove north from Manhattan toward Shandy, he told himself now he could face the Master with confidence. He had at last found the courage to commit a love-death. Now he could look into the Master's eyes certain that his love and devotion would be unquestioned. What a book he could write on murder *now!* And his theories of human nature . . . *all* of them . . . hadn't they all been proved? He looked at the dashboard clock: one-thirty. Raymond had been on Earth over thirty hours now. Norton had briefly wondered why the news had not yet spread—wouldn't the Master herald his arrival with a worldwide mira-cle?

He knew the Master was planning to stay at the Bernsteins' house until the temple could be built, so when he reached the campus he drove there first. The house was dark as he rang the bell. He heard it somewhere in the distance. No one answered. He rang again. Still no one. He kept ringing, at first anxiously, then angrily. Where *were* they? Didn't they know how *eager* he was? Didn't they want to see God? . . . He was confused. He meant, of course, didn't they want him to see God?

Of course. They must all be at the shrine of the martyrs where the Master would be leading them in prayer. Hurrying back to his car, he started toward Ben Scovill's house on the other side of Rock Mountain. What joy to be an apostle in a new religion! Norton had been alone most of his life, but now he would know the joy of fellowship, the sweetness of belonging to a communion of souls. Loneliness would be banished forever now, because for the rest of time *he* would be one with the Master. The Master one with him.

As he parked in front of the dark, sagging farmhouse, he wondered if the others had walked up the mountain. There were no cars. Perhaps it had been a pilgrimage? A candlelight procession to the mountaintop? Oh, if he had missed that, he would never forgive himself. Taking a flashlight from the glove compartment, he hurried out of the car and ran up on the sagging porch.

He touched the front door and it squeaked slowly open. Following the beam of his flashlight, he hurried into the kitchen. He stopped for a moment as the eyes of a rat reflected the light back at him. The rat scurried into the shadows, and Norton tugged open the trapdoor.

He turned on the light switch, recalling the pleasure he and Jack had experienced arranging the shrine, dressing the corpses, placing the roses in the women's hands. . . . He started down the steps. But where were they? Where were the apostles? For that matter, where were the martyrs? The coffins were as empty as the cellar.